THE
SCOWLING
FROG

NOVELS FOR ADULT LEARNERS

THE
SCOWLING
FROG

KATE FERRIS

CENTRE FOR CURRICULUM, TRANSFER AND TECHNOLOGY
VICTORIA, BRITISH COLUMBIA

THE SCOWLING FROG
by Kate Ferris
Copyright © 1997 by the Province of British Columbia
Ministry of Education, Skills and Training
All rights reserved.

This novel has been written especially for adults learners improving their reading skills.
The development and production was funded by the Province of British Columbia,
Ministry of Education, Skills and Training and Human Resources Development Canada,
National Literacy Secretariat.

Project coordination: Centre for Curriculum, Transfer and Technology
Design and production coordination: Bendall Books
Cover design and illustration: Bernadette Boyle

CANADIAN CATALOGUING IN PUBLICATION DATA
Ferris, Kate.
    The scowling frog
    (Novels for adult learners)
    ISBN 0-7718-9490-2
    1. High interest-low vocabulary books. 2. Readers
(Adult) I. Centre for Curriculum, Transfer and
Technology. II. Title. III. Series.
PS8561.E7S36 1997   428'.62   C97-960063-4
PR9199.3F4S36 1997

NOVELS FOR ADULT LEARNERS	ORDER NO.	ISBN
The Buckle by Don Sawyer	VA0190	0-7718-9493-7
Crocodiles and Rivers by Don Sawyer	VA0191	0-7718-9492-9
Frozen Tears by Don Sawyer	VA0192	0-7718-9491-0
The Mailbox by Kate Ferris	VA0193	0-7718-9488-0
The Scowling Frog by Kate Ferris	VA0194	0-7718-9490-2
Three Wise Men by Kate Ferris	VA0195	0-7718-9489-9
Package of 6 Novels	CPUB130M	0-7719-1757-0
Activities Handbook for Instructors	VA0276	0-7718-9557-7

ORDERING

Distributed By:
Grass Roots Press
Toll Free: 1-888-303-3213
Fax: (780) 413-6582
Web Site: www.literacyservices.com

)-356-2820 or 1-888-883-4766
120
ications@gems5.gov.bc.ca
lications.gov.bc,ca
order (no personal cheques)
...astercard, including expiry date.

Acknowledgements

This book was written in consultation with the Adult Basic Education classes at the Selkirk College Learning Centre in Nakusp, B.C. The meetings with the students were immensely enjoyable and fruitful. I thank them all.

Special thanks go to Patty Bossort, who initiated this project; also to Richard Allin, Susan Crichton; and to Craig Anderson at Selkirk College.

I would also like to thank Audrey Thomas, Yvette Souque, Dennis Anderson, and JoAnne Pasquale and their respective agencies.

*T*he boat tips its nose to the sky. It is an old whaleboat, 24 feet long. The engine sputters, choked by the waves. It is a 1928 Star engine. It is doing its best. In the open boat, there is no cabin, no place to hide. Up, up, the bow of the boat is lifted on the huge wave. Then it plunges steeply down into the sea again, as if aiming straight to the bottom.

They should have known better. They should have feared the body of water called the Queen Charlotte Strait. They should have known that the sea would punish anyone caught stealing.

1

THE WHALEBOAT

July 1966

As the plane circled to land, Alice peered out the small oval window. Below, the island spun slowly.

This was Canada. This was the wilderness. Below lay the airport at Sandspit. All she could see was a few houses and stores, a hotel. The long runway came into view. The plane levelled itself. The landing gear locked into place with a loud "Clunk!"

Alice sat back in her seat. She closed her eyes. She had seen him, down there: Nathan. A tiny figure waving its arms.

Her heart started pounding. She reached for her purse. Her hands shook as she opened her pink frosted lipstick. In the small mirror her dark eyes blinked back at her. She pressed her lips together. The plane landed with a bump. The brakes screamed, the engines roared as the DC-3 slowed to a final, safe stop.

Alice was afraid of flying. She had worried during the flight up from Seattle to Vancouver. But on the flight over from Vancouver she'd been calm. The plane couldn't crash. Her excitement alone would keep the plane in the air.

Nathan's photo had lain in her lap the whole trip. She stared at the photo now, at Nathan's soft mouth, his dark beard. His eyes looked out at her from behind thick glasses. His last postcard had been signed "Love." No, that wasn't true. He had only signed "Love ya."

Alice unbuckled her seat belt. She stood up, and smoothed her new blue dress over her hips. Her hips were wide, too wide. She knew that. But for once she had dared to wear a tight dress. She hoped Nathan would like it. What if he didn't? What if he thought she was too fat? What if he didn't want her here, after all? What if she was in the way?

The ladder leading down from the plane was steep. Alice gripped the railing. The wind blew her hair across her eyes. She couldn't see.

"Alice!"

She turned her head.

"Alice!"

Then she was running. She ran towards the chain-link fence. It was a tall fence, eight feet high. Behind it stood two men. They pressed their bodies into the fence. Their fingers clutched the metal links. They looked like two caged animals. But smiles were on their unshaven faces. Big smiles.

Nathan watched Alice run towards him. She was beautiful. A tall, big, beautiful girl. He must have been crazy to leave her behind. He must be crazy to have let her come! Look at her, wearing high heels and a dress, out here in the bush. Then Alice stopped. She took off her high heel shoes. She held them in one hand as she ran barefoot across the pavement.

Nathan had met Alice two months ago. And one month ago he had left Seattle. Late one evening, he had steered a small whale-boat out of the harbour. With his hand on the tiller, the boat had headed north into open water. Leaving behind the lights of the city. And leaving Alice behind.

And now, here she was. As she ran towards him the wind flattened her dress against her curves. It blew her hair across her face. Five feet away, she stopped. She turned shy. "Hello."

"Come here," he said. "Closer."

She took a step.

"Closer." He pressed his face against the chain-link fence.

She took another step, and leaned forward. Through an opening in the metal links, they kissed.

It was a sweet, polite kiss. Nathan came from a "good" family. He was the youngest son. But he was the black sheep. At 18, he had left his parents' house in New York and hitch-hiked to Seattle. He'd grown a beard, and let his hair grow long. And now here he was, two years later, about to become a hero, and a thief.

The kiss lasted a long, sweet moment. Then Alice drew back. She blushed.

"I guess I don't get a kiss." The man who spoke had a gold front tooth. He stood next to Nathan at the chain-link fence. He needed a shave. The wind blew his thinning hair across his bald spot.

Nathan turned to him. "Sorry! I forgot you were here." Then Nathan turned to the girl on the other side of the fence. "Alice, I want you to meet Harry Pozzi. Pozzi, this is Alice."

"How do ya? Sorry we can't shake hands." But he poked a dirty finger through the fence.

Alice laughed. She shook his finger.

Harry Pozzi grinned at Nathan. His gold tooth flashed in the sun. "You got a nice girl here, kid."

The three of them walked through the town. The warm wind lifted dust into their eyes. Scraps of paper swirled in the air. Above the few buildings, seagulls rode the gusts of wind. Their cries seemed to exclaim over Alice below in her blue dress.

When the three reached the path along the bay, Nathan took the lead. "I'll go first."

Nathan was four years younger than Alice. But she had followed him here, to the Queen Charlotte Islands. She followed him now, along this narrow dirt path. Nathan's hair hung long at the back of his neck. He carried her small suitcase. A green backpack hung from his shoulder. Alice wondered what was in it. Lunch? She was hungry. Sure, she had extra fat on her hips. But her stomach was empty.

The path curved along the shore. On her left, the bank rose into thick forest. On her right, the water slapped at the sandy coves.

Water reeds leaned in the strong breeze. But when she rounded a bend in the path, the wind quieted. Alice could now hear the sounds of the wild. Birdcalls, and the chatter of squirrels.

Far across the water, to the north, mountains rose up. Alice knew that what looked like a lake was just a wide channel between two islands. Before leaving Seattle she had studied a map of British Columbia. On the map, the Queen Charlotte Islands looked so remote, they looked like they were floating out to sea.

So Alice knew that this body of water was, in truth, seawater. It was an inlet from the sea. But she pretended it was a lake. A lake, with no wind blowing, just the warm sun shining down. She was finally here, with Nathan. If she stretched out her arm, she could touch his back. She could smell him. He smelled of wood smoke and tobacco. He smelled good.

To the right of the path, ducks bobbed on the gently lifting water. You would never know there was anything to fear from the sea. You would never guess that in a few short minutes, a breeze could blow into a gale.

A crash through the underbrush warned of a huge animal—a bear or an elk! Not the tiny deer that now leapt across the path and struggled up the slope.

"It was just a fawn!" Alice cried in relief.

"Hell, that was a grand-daddy." said Pozzi.

"But it was so small!"

"That's an island deer. They… " But then Pozzi shut up. Let Nathan be the big shot.

Nathan picked up the story. "The deer are small because there are so many of them. There's only so much space, and so much food."

Nathan's voice droned on. Pozzi wasn't listening. He was walking behind Alice. His eyes followed the sway of her hips. The blue dress pulled tight over her nice big bottom as she walked. It had been a long time, way too long, since he'd been with a woman. The loneliness made his spirits sink. He remembered the long nights of driving taxi in Seattle. He remembered coming home at dawn to Grace, and finding her passed out, drunk. Sometimes Pozzi would find a strange man in the bed—who got out fast.

Then the quarreling with Grace would start. Sometimes Pozzi would get drunk himself. But sometimes he would end it. "I gotta get some sleep, Grace." And he would turn his back to her tears.

The last time he'd spoken to Grace was the night he left Seattle. He phoned her from the docks. The phone rang once, twice. Then, "Who is it?" He heard the booze in her voice.

"It's me," he said. "Did you see the doctor?"

"Yeah, I saw the doctor. Turns out I got cancer. Now you happy?" And she hung up.

That was a month ago. So that's how long it was, since he'd been with a woman. And a pain had chewed at him ever since. The pain was his worry about Grace.

Women are trouble. Last night he had told Nathan just that. "Why bring your girlfriend up here? It's better that no one knows what we're up to."

"But we aren't doing anything wrong."

"Tell that to the RCMP. Tell it to the Haida! If the Indians find out…"

"This trip was your idea."

Pozzi sighed. "Yes, it was my idea." Then he smiled up at Nathan. "And it's gonna make us rich."

In front of him on the path, Alice stopped short. Pozzi almost bumped into her.

"You okay?" he asked. There was a patch of mud ahead on the path.

Alice looked down at her bare toes. "Sure I'm okay." She still carried her high heels in one hand. She hesitated only for a moment, then walked lightly through the mud. She called ahead to Nathan, "Where are we going?"

"Nowhere. We're here." Nathan slid down the bank to the shore. He held out a hand to Alice: "Jump." She jumped, and landed on the sand beside him. Their faces were inches apart. Pozzi looked down at them. The girl was waiting for another kiss.

But Nathan turned. He pointed towards the reeds: "There she is."

"Who?"

"Our boat." A boat was hidden among the water reeds. "She brought us up from Seattle, and she'll take us back." Pride was in Nathan's voice. "It's an old whaling boat. Look—this is where they stored the harpoons."

"You came all the way up from Seattle in *this*?"

Nathan glanced up at Pozzi. Their eyes met. Pozzi answered for him. "Yup."

The two men waded into the water. They pulled the boat from its hiding place among the reeds.

Alice waded after them. "Shall I get in now?" She felt her stomach growl with hunger. She waded in farther, up to her knees. The hem of her blue dress was wet. She stood there, and waited. The water was chilly.

The boat seemed to be drifting away from her. The two men bent over a large wooden box in the centre of the boat. This was the housing for the engine. The lid was off. The engine was giving them trouble. At last, it sparked to life. A cloud of fumes rose into the clear air.

And Alice was not left behind, after all. She sat on top of the engine box. Her small suitcase sat next to her. The vibration of the engine caused her whole body to tremble. The engine's noise was muffled by the lid.

The bow of the boat pointed into the channel, and then headed west, along the shoreline. A family of ducks swam ahead of the boat. The boat was gaining on the ducks. "Look out!" shouted Alice. Her warning was meant for the men behind her, steering the boat. But it was the mother duck who veered to one side. All her little ducklings tried to catch up.

The boat followed the shoreline. Alice looked back over her shoulder at the two men. Pozzi was at the tiller, steering the wooden handle with one hand. Nathan sat on the bench. He gripped a can of tobacco between his knees. He was rolling a cigarette. Pozzi watched Nathan's fingers. "Use your thumbs," he said. "That's right."

Pozzi struck a match. The two men lit up.

The strong smoke reached Alice's nose. "That smells awful."

The men smoked in silence. Finally, Alice ventured to ask, "Where are we going?"

"Home," was the answer.

Home was a little floathouse, owned by a logging company. The little house floated in the middle of a cove. A long, floating dock ran out to it from the shore.

The house itself sat on a raft. A person could walk all around the little shack, and look over the side, down into the green water.

Nathan tied the boat to one of the posts on the floating dock. With every step, the dock tilted, side to side. He crossed to the raft, and the little shack. No key needed. He pushed open the door. The place was empty, except for two beds, and a table and chairs. He set his backpack on the table. On one of the beds he laid Alice's suitcase. This was his bed. It was narrow. It was meant to sleep one person. But it would hold them both.

From the window he could see Alice. She was outside, looking over the edge of the raft. He knew what Alice was seeing: the depths of the dark green water. Nathan knew it was deep in this cove, very deep. And he knew that he wanted to be alone with her.

When Alice came through the door he was glad. He didn't show it. Instead, he opened his backpack. He pulled out a carton of eggs, and a can of maple syrup. Then a can of beans. And some cigarette papers.

Alice looked at all this. "What are we having for dinner? Syrup on beans?" But it was no joke. She was hungry. "Is this the food cupboard?" She opened it. Inside was flour, salt and coffee.

Nathan reached to the bottom of the backpack. He pulled out a loaf of bread, a can of Spam, a tin of sardines, and a few more cans of beans. "That's it," he said. "That will feed us for a few days." He didn't tell Alice the truth: that he had only five dollars left.

It was very quiet in the little house. They looked at each other. The table was between them.

Nathan walked around the table. He put his arms around Alice's waist. He kissed her. A good long kiss.

When he drew back, Alice smiled. "I'm not hungry anymore."

At that moment they jumped apart as Pozzi kicked the door open. He carried a big armload of sticks. He dropped a small ax, and dumped the firewood to the floor with a clatter. "Who's cooking tonight?"

Then he looked at Nathan. He looked at Alice. Alice blushed.

"Oh. Sorry," said Pozzi. He rubbed a hand over his rough cheeks. "Guess I'll go shave before dinner."

And he backed out the door.

For dinner, Alice ate four big pancakes. Nathan stood at the wood stove. "Do you want another one?" He held a fork over the frying pan. "No? What about you, Pozzi?"

Pozzi shook his head. He had eaten only a single pancake. "My stomach doesn't feel good. My ulcer is acting up."

Nathan forked the pancake onto his own plate. He sat down and ate. He was waiting for dark.

Pozzi must have read Nathan's thoughts. He pulled out his pocketwatch. "Seven o'clock." It was still light outside. It was high summer. Three more hours till bed.

Alice spoke up. "Do you have a pack of cards?"

Pozzi looked at her in surprise. "You know how to play poker?"

"Nope," she answered.

"You know how to play gin rummy?"

"Nope."

Pozzi sighed. "What games *do* you know?"

"I know Go Fish."

Pozzi brought out his cards. He pushed aside their plates. "I'll teach you to play poker."

Nathan gathered the plates from the table. "I'll wash the dishes."

Outside, Nathan kneeled down at the edge of the raft. He dipped the dirty plates into the water, and the three forks. The sun was low in the evening sky. Then he sat back against the wall of the floathouse. He rolled a cigarette.

Seattle was far away. New York was even farther. His parents didn't know he was in Canada. No one did, not even the border patrol. He and Pozzi had left Seattle's harbour in the dark, with no lights on the boat. They had slipped across into Canadian waters. And if they were lucky, they could slip back into the States the same way. He told himself that there was no need to worry. No need.

He could hear Alice's laughter from inside. He wanted to go in and lift that blue dress over her head. Take it off.

At nine o'clock they lit the candles. Nathan tried to read. He sat on his bed in the corner. Alice and Pozzi were still playing poker.

At one point, Pozzi muttered, "Boy, I could sure use a drink."

Nathan called across the room, "You're on the wagon."

"Yeah, you're right. I'm on the wagon." Pozzi looked at the cards in his hands. Then he looked across the table at Alice. He had to boast: "I haven't had a drink since we left Seattle. One month!"

At 10 o'clock, Pozzi stood up. He stretched his arms over his head. He yawned. "It's time for an old man like me to be in bed."

They blew the candles out. They all undressed in the dark. On the other side of the room, Pozzi climbed into his sleeping bag.

Nathan lifted up his own sleeping bag from the bed. He drew its zipper open. In a low voice he said, "Lie down. I'll put my sleeping bag over you." And then, at long last, he lay down next to Alice.

He turned to her. In the dark, her skin felt so warm.

Alice whispered, "We can't do anything yet."

"Why not?"

"Because Pozzi will hear."

So they waited. They lay face to face in the dark. Nathan could feel the floathouse swaying. He pressed his mouth to her ear. "I missed you." He kissed her neck.

"Wait," Alice whispered.

Finally, they heard a snore. And another. Pozzi was snoring. He was asleep.

Nathan rolled on top of Alice. She lay under him. Their noses touched. Their breath mingled.

He pressed his mouth down on her mouth, as they began to make love.

But it was happening too quickly. And then before he could stop himself, he gasped. His head tilted back. He gasped again.

It was over.

Nathan dropped his head to Alice's shoulder. He lay there, on top of her. He closed his eyes. He wanted to say that he was sorry. He wanted to tell her that next time it would be better.

But he didn't say anything. His body grew heavy. He tried to spare her his full weight. But sleep overtook him, and he let go. He was floating. His face was in her hair.

Face down, he floated on a soft, warm sea.

*A*nother wave lifts the whaleboat. On the bottom of the boat lie the Sun, and Raven, and Scowling Frog. They are wrapped in canvas. The canvas is like a blindfold. They can't see where they are being taken. But they can sense the waves rising in protest under the boat. They know where they are, and they are not afraid.

The two men are screaming at each other. They are trying to be heard above the wind's howl.

"There's only two life jackets!"

"What?!"

"Two, I said! Only two life jackets in the box!"

And in the boat there are three people.

2

THE SCOWLING FROG

Alice opened her eyes. It was morning. Nathan was standing near the foot of the bed. He stood with his back to her. He was naked. There was no fat on his body, none. Only lean muscle.

He bent to pull on his baggy pants. He pulled them up over his buttocks. The pants were a dull green. They were old army pants. He pulled his sweater on over his head. The sweater was baggy too. There were holes at the elbows.

And yet Nathan came from a good family, a family with money. Of course, Nathan didn't say they were rich. The word "rich" was not a word used by the rich. They were "well-off."

Nathan sat down on the edge of the bed. He pulled on his socks. He didn't realize she was awake.

Alice lay still, watching him. Nathan was only 20 years old, but somehow he seemed much older. He knew what he wanted. He wanted never to be tied down—to a job, to a wife.

He leaned across the bed. His glasses were on the window sill. His arm stretched across Alice's legs. His fingers closed around his glasses.

"I'm awake," she said.

Nathan jerked back. He squinted down at her. "I was going to make a fire." He had weak eyes, he was almost blind without his glasses. He put them on. Then he ran his fingers through his beard to comb it. He smoothed his long hair back. He looked around. "Where's my cap?"

Alice's heart sank. Nathan didn't want to be with her. He wouldn't look her in the eye. She tried to keep her voice level. "Before I forget, will you hand my purse to me?"

He found it under the bed, and handed it over.

"Birth control pill," she explained.

He looked sheepish. He must be remembering last night. "Do you need a glass of water?"

"No. I just swallow it dry."

"I better go make a fire."

Soon, the scent of wood smoke drifted over to Alice. The fire crackled in the stove.

When the smell of frying Spam filled the room, Pozzi sat up in his bed. His thin hair stuck out from his head in all directions. "What time is it?"

"Wait!" cried Alice, "I have to get dressed."

So Pozzi turned over, and faced the wall.

Alice jumped naked from the bed. She grabbed her underwear,

and her jeans and a shirt from her suitcase. She dressed as fast as she could. She had to pee.

Outside, the salt air greeted her. The water lapped at the raft. She couldn't pee off the raft. She hurried along the floating dock till she reached the shore. She didn't dare go into the forest. Behind a large bush, she pulled down her jeans, and squatted. It was a strange thing: she felt sad. In this beautiful place, with birds singing, tears ran down her face. She ripped a few leaves from the bush, to use as toilet paper. She pulled up her jeans. She could sense the tall trees staring down at her from the forest. It made her uneasy.

She ran back along the swaying dock.

Nathan and Pozzi were looking at a map on the table. They'd spread the map open all the way, pushing their dirty plates to one side. They didn't look up.

Alice helped herself to breakfast. Nathan had toasted bread on top of the wood stove. Toast, with a slice of fried Spam on top. She sat on the edge of the bed to eat. Her fingers dripped grease from the Spam. She had never tasted anything so good.

Over at the table, the two men spoke in low voices.

"Where are we going?" asked Alice, with her mouth full.

Nathan lifted his head. "What? Oh. Fishing. We're going fishing."

"Yeah," said Pozzi. "Fishing."

"But we need you to stay here, Alice. A tugboat is due to arrive today. We don't want them to leave without us." Nathan was finally looking straight at her.

"I have to stay here by myself?" Alice tried not to whine.

"Just tell the captain that we'll be ready when he is. He's going to tow us back."

"Tow us where?" Alice was now confused.

"As far as Vancouver Island. A tow will be faster. And we'll save on gas."

Alice chewed the last bite of toast. She swallowed. It took a long time going down her throat. Then she asked, "How long will you be gone fishing?"

The men looked at each other across the table. "Three hours," said Nathan. "Four," said Pozzi.

Nathan waved from the stern of the boat. Alice waved back. The whaleboat headed west through the channel. She waved again, but there was no answering wave. They could have left a note for the tugboat captain. And she, Alice, could now be in that boat with the men, going fishing.

Why? Why had Nathan wanted to get away from her?

She went inside. The breakfast dishes were still on the table. Why was she even here? Why had she flown all the way up from Seattle to wash dishes?

She grabbed a towel from her suitcase, and shampoo.

Outside in the warm sunshine she stripped to her bra and panties. There was no one to see her. No one to tell her she was too big, too tall, too loud. She hooted at the blue sky. She turned to look across the water at the shore and the forest. She yelled as loudly as she could, "ANYBODY HOME?"

The silence that followed was quickly filled with birdsong. A squirrel began chattering from the limb of a tree. He scolded her. But Alice felt better.

At the edge of the raft, she dipped a toe into the water. Cold, but not too cold. She kneeled down. Bending her head over the side, she wet her hair. Then she rubbed in shampoo, and dipped her head again.

There was salt left in her hair from the seawater. She toweled it dry. Soap bubbles drifted across the water of the cove. Alice watched them drift, and blink themselves gone. She was alone here.

She lay back on the raft. She turned her head towards the shore, towards the forest. She was safe as long as she stayed on the raft. Along the shore, the dark green trees grew thick and close together. Alice knew that there were secrets hidden beyond that first row of trees. Behind them, the forest opened into its own darkness.

She had never dared to explore her own secret dreams. For six years Alice had worked at a dull, safe job in Seattle. She was a file clerk. But what did she really want?

Lying on the raft in the sun, she hummed a little tune.

She turned on her side, and rested her head on her hands. Her hands were pressed together under her head, as if in prayer. She stared across the water, towards those dark trees.

She wasn't prepared for what happened next.

Between the shore and where she lay on the raft, a huge, finned shape surfaced. It was black and white. Its smooth back curved into the water and was gone.

Alice blinked. A small wave hit the raft, rocking it.

Then, before she could move, it happened again. This time, two blunt heads surfaced. Alice saw a small black eye. It looked directly at her.

The two huge creatures humped their backs. Two fins flashed past, and went under. The water closed over them.

The visit had happened with hardly a sound. A few small waves slapped the side of the raft.

Alice didn't move. She waited. She felt as if the creatures had spoken to her. But was that all? Would they come back?

Pozzi rolled two cigarettes. He sat on the engine box, facing backwards, towards the stern of the boat. He licked his tongue along the tube of a cigarette, and glued the paper closed. "These are going to kill us someday," he said. He lit the cigarette for Nathan.

Nathan leaned forward and stretched out his fingers. He kept one hand on the tiller. He was steering the boat farther west through the inlet.

"Thanks." He sat back, and raised the cigarette to his lips. He drew the smoke deeply into his lungs. Pozzi watched him. Nathan's dark cap had two long ribbons hanging down the side. It was a sailor's cap. Pozzi didn't know what country's navy the cap was from. It didn't matter. Nathan acted as if he was free of any country, and damned free of any country's navy. The kid was just like Pozzi used to be: he didn't believe that he could ever die.

Dying only happened to other people. It wouldn't happen to him.

Pozzi took a last deep puff of his own cigarette, and flicked the butt over the side of the boat. The butt quickly floated out of sight. Behind them, the boat's wake stretched off into the distance. On the north side of the boat, and on the south, the forest seemed to move closer. The channel was narrowing. It was as if time was running out. Pozzi looked at Nathan. "Kid, there's something I haven't told you. It's about Grace."

"Who's Grace?"

"Grace? She's my old lady."

"You're married?"

"Hell no!"

Pozzi fell silent after that. The engine box vibrated under him as the boat moved west. The channel here was shallow. Sand beaches moved slowly past. This should be one of the best days of his life. But his stomach hurt.

Nathan called to him over the noise of the engine. "What were you going to tell me?"

"Oh, it was nothing. I just have stuff on my mind."

"Like what?"

Pozzi's mouth twisted into a painful grin. "Grace has cancer. She told me just before we left Seattle. I didn't want to say anything." Before Nathan could reply, Pozzi went on. "Yeah. It's probably in her lungs. She smokes even more than I do." He ran a hand over his thinning hair. Then he squinted north, at the shoreline.

"I'm sorry, Pozzi."

"Yeah." He couldn't look at Nathan. Instead, Pozzi pointed. "There's that boulder we saw before. I think we're getting close."

The boulder on the shore was cracked down the middle. A small cedar tree grew out of the crack.

The water was choppy now. They were getting closer to the mouth of the channel, and the open sea. The boat rocked on the waves.

Pozzi stood up. He shaded his eyes with his hand. "Yup. We're here. There's our stones."

They had marked this beach with a pile of stones. It was far up from the water, out of reach of the tide. Driftwood was scattered over the sand. The beach sloped up into thick brush.

Pozzi shut off the engine. Nathan steered the whaleboat towards the beach. The bow scraped onto the sand. Pozzi leapt out, and tied the boat to a big log of driftwood. He called to Nathan, "Bring the saw with you."

Up beyond the beach, thick bushes formed a wall of green. Pozzi walked up to their pile of stones. He shouted to Nathan, "Here's the path!"

Pozzi forgot about the pain in his stomach. He rolled his sleeves down, and began pushing his way through stinging nettles. They grew higher than his head. The limbs slapped at his face. He fought his way through, lifting his arms in front of him. The forest didn't want them here. They were strangers. They were white men.

These bushes and trees had known only the Haida people. For over 7,000 years, the sand beaches had welcomed the giant canoes. Along the shore, tall poles had faced the sea. On the poles, the carved and painted faces of Eagle and Bear, Salmon and Beaver had stared out across the water. Beneath the totem poles there had lived a village: men and women and children. Dogs snatching at drying fish. A carver working his knife into a new pole. The big houses of the village had been built of cedar logs and cedar planks. The houses had lined the beach in a single row, facing out to the sea.

Pozzi had seen the old photographs, taken in 1884, and in 1901. For long hours he had stared at them in the Seattle Library. He had stared at the faces of the Haida people. And at their great houses. Each house boasted a tall totem pole by the front door. What had it been like to live in the shadow of these poles? They reached to the sky.

Sitting in the library, he had wondered: Was anything left of the villages? Of the poles? What was left now, in 1966?

What was here now were nettles, grown over the old village site. Pozzi fought the thick brush, pushing his way through. Two weeks ago, he and Nathan had been here. They had hacked a path. But the nettles grew fast. They had already grown back, as if by magic.

Pozzi beat them down again. He didn't believe in ghosts. He didn't believe in spirits. He pushed his way through the nettles and emerged into the forest. Nathan was behind him. Pozzi turned to him, "Do you have the saw?"

"Yes, of course I have the saw."

Cedar and hemlock trees towered above them. These were young trees, only 50 or 60 years old.

Old totem poles leaned among the trees. Vines wrapped around the faces of Bear and Whale and Beaver. Moss clutched the fins and claws carved into the wood long ago. Some of the poles had broken off, halfway up.

Pozzi squinted up at one of the broken poles. Vines and moss grew from the top of a woman's head. The woman had only one arm. Her breasts were two eagle heads, with curved, sharp beaks.

Some of the poles had leaned so far that they'd toppled and fallen. They lay among brush and vines. They were rotting into the soil. This was their burial ground.

Pozzi knew what he was looking at: money. His heart pounded. Lots of money. These totems were works of art. There were people in Seattle who would pay a lot for what lay rotting at his feet. "Hand me the saw."

Above his head, the poles leaned this way and that way. They looked as if they were drunk, or too old to stay on their feet. The vines that twined around the poles seemed to be trying to keep them upright.

Pozzi walked over to one of the leaning poles. "Let's take this one."

But as he started sawing, Nathan jumped him. "Don't do that!"

And he grabbed the saw from Pozzi's hand. "You said we would only cut up the poles that were fallen."

"Hell. One more year or so, this pole is going to fall anyway. Look at this face!" He leaned closer. "Look here—he still has some teeth." It was the face of a bear, carved into the wood. Real bear's teeth had once lined his open mouth. A few of the sharp white teeth remained.

Pozzi stared up at the bear's carved face. Green moss filled the small, cupped ears. Both eyes had deep cracks down the center, from old age. There was no paint left on the wood. Rain and wind and sand had worn off all colour. It was a grey face, but still fierce. It stared back.

A chill ran through Pozzi. He shivered, and took a step backward. "Okay, okay. You win. Now give me back the saw."

But Nathan had found something within a circle of cedar saplings. The young trees had been hiding an old grey totem from view. The Frog squatted in the dirt. He was all that was left of a pole. His wide mouth turned down in a scowl.

Nathan began sawing down the saplings. A branch knocked his cap off. He picked it up and set it back on his head. A little later his glasses were knocked off. Nathan froze. Blindly he felt around with his hands until he found them. The saplings were fighting him.

As Nathan cut down each of the cedar saplings, Pozzi dragged them out of the way. Finally, all the saplings were down. The totem had nowhere to hide.

Pozzi stood in front of the Frog. He braced his legs. He wrapped his arms around the totem, and pulled. Nothing happened. The Frog, the base of the pole, was rooted deep in the earth.

"Give me the saw," said Pozzi.

Nathan looked at him. Then he squatted down, just like the Frog. "Maybe we shouldn't take it." He studied the old grey face, with its scowl.

"Give me the saw," Pozzi said again.

"No." Nathan stood up. He pushed his glasses up on his nose.

"Nathan, I need this frog. He's going to pay for Grace's doctor bills. And he's going to pay for a ring. A wedding ring. I'm going to marry Grace. Hell, she's nagged me long enough about it."

Nathan stared down at the carved frog, its wood grey and cracked. "I'm sorry that I even found it."

"Yeah, I know you're sorry."

Pozzi set the sharp teeth of the saw against the base of the totem. He began sawing under the Frog's webbed feet.

Nathan slapped at mosquitoes. Standing on the beach, he slapped his neck, and his cheek. The mosquitoes had followed him down from the old village site. They had followed him through the thick undergrowth of nettles. They hovered around his neck and ears. They hummed. They tortured him. They joined with the hum of his own thoughts. He couldn't be rid of them. He'd had a sense of being followed, each time he'd carried out a totem.

Now he slapped at his hand, killing six mosquitoes at once. He wiped the drops of blood on his pants.

"Come on!" Pozzi yelled from the boat. All the totems were now packed in the boat. There was no reason to stay.

The cloud of mosquitoes hovered about Nathan's face, his hands, his clothes. As he slapped at them, he kept staring back over his shoulder.

"You're just spooked," Pozzi yelled. "Come into the boat. The mosquitoes will quit, once we get out into the channel."

Nathan stood where he was. Only his arms moved, slapping at the insects. He was looking back at the old Haida village site. Above it, high in the air, two ravens circled. They flapped their wings, then glided, round and round. What were they seeing, that he couldn't see?

"Nathan!"

Pozzi's sharp call broke the spell. Nathan hobbled down across the beach towards the boat. His ankle hurt. He must have twisted it, coming through the underbrush. Now he remembered: something had grabbed at his foot. Maybe a root.

At the water's edge, he leaned his body against the bow of the boat and pushed it off the sand. Small waves were splashing all along the beach. The sea's waves were washing in from the mouth of the inlet to the west. Nathan could hear the surf pounding out there.

He pushed the whaleboat farther into the water. There was a scraping noise as the bottom of the boat was pushed across the pebbles. And then the whaleboat was afloat, bobbing up and down in the small waves. Nathan climbed in. He took care not to step on the totems. They were wrapped in canvas. They lay in front of the engine box, at the bow of the boat. Pozzi had pushed them under the foredeck. There were six of the totems, six large faces wrapped in canvas. Nathan was glad to have them out of sight. He switched on the engine. Pozzi steered as the engine took them out into the channel.

They were underway. Nathan sat on the bench at the middle of the boat. He tried to be calm. He picked burrs and leaves off his sweater. His hands stung from the nettles. His neck itched from the bites of the mosquitoes. At least *they* were now left behind, out here in the breeze of the channel. But whatever had been following him was still following. How long would this feeling persist?

"Pozzi, did you have the feeling that someone was watching us, back there?"

Pozzi's voice boomed out: "The whole damn village was watching us!"

"What do you mean? There was no one there."

Pozzi grinned. His gold tooth glinted in the sun as he steered. "If there was no one there, why are you spooked?" He leaned forward and patted Nathan's knee. "Kid, you're learning, you're learning."

And then he leaned back, one hand still on the tiller. He couldn't wipe that silly grin off his face. "Now is the time I'd have a drink. If I wasn't on the wagon," he added. He gave Nathan's foot a kick. "Hey, we did it! Think of it as a rescue mission. Those totems were just rotting in the woods."

"What about Alice?" said Nathan.

"What about her?"

"Shall I… " Nathan cleared his throat. "Shall I tell her what we're doing?"

"Kid, she doesn't want to know. She's in love with you. She wants to believe that you're perfect. She doesn't want to know that you're doing something against the law."

"But we might get caught, at the border. I'm putting her in danger."

"No one's going to get caught. By the end of the week, we'll all be back in Seattle. You know what? I'm thinking of buying a new taxi as well. We're going to get a lot of money for that frog."

Nathan shuddered. He didn't want to think about the frog, lying hidden under canvas at the bow of the boat. "Why a new taxi, Pozzi? Can't you fix the damage to your old one?"

"That accident wasn't my fault. I told the insurance company to go to hell."

"Pozzi, you were drunk when you ran into that bridge!"

"Who told you that?"

"*You* did."

"Yeah. I guess I must have. What a mess."

The boat moved east through the channel, away from the open sea. The waves smoothed out. Only the chugging of the engine sounded as they headed back to the floathouse. Pozzi was at the tiller. Nathan sat facing him, but his thoughts were elsewhere. *I lied to Alice.* Aloud he muttered, "I told her we were going fishing."

"Who, Alice?"

"Yes."

"Well, get out the line!"

But Nathan didn't move from the bench. He was thinking of Alice, and last night in bed. His face flushed in shame. He'd wanted to make love to her for hours. And it had all been over in less than a minute. Sitting in the boat, his cheeks burned.

"Look what we've got here!" Pozzi steered the boat towards the shore. They had reached the deeper part of the channel. But the tide was pulling out, leaving a mudflat below the beach. A heron stalked through the mud on its long legs. Seagulls filled the air, as other gulls picked their way along the muddy shore.

Pozzi stood up in the boat. "Cut the motor!" He pointed. "See those gulls? They're after mussels." He looked down at Nathan. "Kid, you can forget the fishing line."

Alice came out to greet them. She waited at the door of the float-house as Nathan tied the boat to the dock.

Then she stepped over onto the dock, barefoot. She peered into the bucket that Pozzi held out.

"Mussels. As fresh as you will ever eat," he boasted.

"How do we cook them?"

"Just boil up some seawater and throw them in."

Alice turned to greet Nathan. "I made biscuits. They're cold now, but we can heat them up. Wait… You have stuff in your beard." She picked off bits of leaf. Their eyes met. Then Nathan looked away.

Alice spoke in a rush, "I have something to tell you."

He was already walking towards the floathouse. "I'm sorry we took so long."

"Why are you limping?" she called.

Inside, Nathan was sitting on the bed. He took off his boot. Alice came to sit beside him. "Something happened to me today, Nathan. Something wonderful." She looked into his face. "I saw a dolphin today. I saw *two*. They came right up out of the water next to me. They came to visit."

Nathan pulled off his other boot. "What did they look like?"

Alice told him.

"Was the fin straight up, or did it hook back?"

Alice thought for a moment. "Straight up, I think."

"Those were killer whales, not dolphins."

"Killer whales. Oh."

It wasn't what he had said. It was the way he had said it. Alice bit her lip.

Nathan took off his glasses. He was cleaning them. Without his glasses, everything was a blur. Alice's face was a blur. He didn't have to see her hurt look.

He took a long time cleaning his glasses. He rubbed at them with his sweater for the longest time.

Scowling Frog squats in the bow of the whaleboat. His anger is slow-burning. He was carved to last for many, many years. His life has been long. Already he has outlived the Haida Indian he honors.

Scowling Frog was carved in memory of a single man, a Haida fisherman who was drowned at sea. Scowling Frog remembers him as a man who was sometimes foolish. A man who sometimes boasted. But a man whose heart was as soft as a boy's.

3

Skunk Cabbage

After dinner, Nathan was restless. He paced the room. It was still early.

He stood at the window, looking out. Alice watched him from the corner of her eye. Maybe he was worried about the tugboat. It still hadn't come. She sat on the bed with her knees drawn up. She was pretending to read. It was a book she'd found on the shelf above the bed. The pages showed how to tie knots.

Nathan turned around. "Let's get out of here."

Pozzi lifted his nose out of his book. He was lying on his bed. "You mean, just leave? And not wait for the tug?"

"I mean," Nathan said, "let's take a run over to Queen Charlotte City for a beer." He grabbed the tin of tobacco, and a warm shirt.

Pozzi sat up. "But what about the tugboat? What if we miss them?"

"They won't be coming tonight. It's too late. They'll wait till morning now."

"Maybe we should save our gas for the trip to Seattle."

"Pozzi, we won't need that much gas. We're getting a tow, remember?"

Alice's heart pounded as she listened to their talk. She said nothing. She pretended to be reading the book on knots.

"Alice?"

She looked up.

Nathan held out his hand. "Let's go."

She jumped up, and pulled on her sneakers.

Nathan looked at her thin shirt. "It will get cool. You'll need a coat."

"I didn't bring a coat. I thought it was summer."

"Here, take my jacket."

"But what about you?"

"I won't need it."

It was calm out on the water. Nathan steered. Alice sat beside him at the boat's stern. His leg leaned against hers.

Seagulls followed the progress of the boat, north across Skidegate Inlet.

An osprey hovered high above the water. Pozzi pointed at the big bird. "He's getting ready to dive, Alice. Watch." The osprey tucked its wings, and dove straight down towards the water and entered without a splash.

"He's diving for his supper," said Pozzi. He sat on the boat's middle bench, facing forward.

A moment later the osprey surfaced. He lifted from the water with a fish in his claws. His long wings slowly beat the air. The fish flapped and twisted, caught. "Oh, the poor thing," Alice cried.

"Kill, or be killed," said Pozzi.

"That's cruel."

"Then I'll put it another way. Eat, or be eaten." Pozzi turned around on the bench, to face Alice. "If you don't find food, Nature will eat you herself. You'll be food for worms."

Pozzi was enjoying this. He rolled himself a cigarette. "You eat meat, don't you?"

Alice nodded, "Sometimes."

"But you don't go out with an ax and kill a cow. You buy it at Safeway, wrapped in plastic."

"So?"

"And you're wearing perfume right now. Right?"

Alice blushed. "Yes."

"Yeah, it smells real pretty. And you know what's in that perfume? Ambergris. It comes from a whale. They had to kill the whale to get it. This boat we're riding in, it used to be a whaler. Sometimes there'd be blood an inch deep in the bottom." He grinned at her, but he was talking now to Nathan. "We've all got blood on our hands."

Nathan had suffered Pozzi's boasting in silence. But now he stood up. "Here—take the tiller and steer."

Alice grabbed the wooden handle with both hands.

Nathan climbed past Pozzi and squeezed past the engine box. He grabbed an oar. Then he climbed up onto the foredeck at the bow. Standing, he lifted the oar above his head and held it high, like a long harpoon. "Whale ahoy!" he shouted.

"Nathan!" cried Alice, "You're acting crazy!"

Nathan pretended to take aim. He drew back his shoulder, and flung the oar. Nathan saw it as a harpoon, and in his mind it trailed a long rope as it sped through the air. *The rope hissed behind it. With great speed and force the harpoon traced a long curve towards the water. And the sharp spike pierced the whale's thick blubber and sped deep into its flesh. The boat had crept up on the dozing whale. And now blood spilled onto the smooth green water of the evening.*

Nathan yelled back over his shoulder, "Got him! Right now we're being pulled through the water at high speed. The whale is trying to make his escape. Blood is spewing from his wound. Hold on! If he dives, he'll take us all with him, down to the bottom." Nathan waved his arms. "Blood, everywhere, all over, a red sea!"

He was being cruel to himself. He was trying to show Alice what a bad choice she had made, in loving him. He wasn't a good man. He wasn't even a man. His father was right. He was just a spoiled brat.

The oar he'd thrown lay just ahead, floating on the water.

Pozzi motioned to Alice. "Steer a little to the left. No, the other way. That's it."

Nathan was calmer now. He was kneeling on the foredeck. The totems were directly below, under the foredeck, tucked out of sight under a canvas. A coil of rope hid them further. But if Alice ever asked him what was under the canvas, what could he say? Would he lie?

He leaned over the side of the whaleboat. "Got it!" He lifted the dripping oar from the water.

"Had your fun?" asked Pozzi, as Nathan climbed past him, back to the tiller.

The boat neared the north shore of the inlet. The steep hillsides were dark with the shadows of evening. Mudflats lined the shore, and stumps rose from the mud. It looked like a cemetery.

Alice shuddered. She pulled Nathan's heavy jacket around her shoulders.

As the boat passed the swampy shore, she saw large flowers growing in the ooze: large, bright yellow-green flowers. "How beautiful!" Then, "Ooh—what stinks?"

Pozzi laughed. "What stinks is the same thing that you're calling beautiful. Those are skunk cabbages."

The slope leading up to the pub was bare of trees. Only stumps remained, and mud. There was a plank walkway through the mud, but it was a narrow plank. The three of them were forced to walk one in front of the other, single file.

The stink of the skunk cabbages followed them. Alice held her sleeve over her nose. The shirt's rough cloth held Nathan's smell. She loved that smell. He was walking right behind her. She wanted to feel his hands on her waist.

When she entered the pub, Alice was greeted by the sweet-sour smell of beer. The pub was only half full. Maybe it was too early yet. Or was it a Sunday? She didn't remember what day of the week it was. She had lost track.

The big room was filled with small round tables. Each table was covered with a red cloth. Smoke filled the air.

The three of them sat down at a table near the window. Alice fingered the tablecloth. It was scarred with cigarette burns. She looked around the room. She was in Canada. It seemed as if everyone in the pub was wearing the same heavy shirt—even the women. It was a large and shapeless shirt of red and black squares. A shirt just like the one Alice was wearing around her shoulders.

Full glasses of beer covered the tables where people sat. Alice tried not to stare. The glasses of beer crowded each table from edge to edge. There wasn't room for even one glass more. Alice leaned towards Pozzi. "Are they really going to drink all that?"

Pozzi nodded, "You bet."

"But why don't they just order one glass at a time?"

"Because, with a full table of beer, they feel rich. It's all ahead of them, all that beer."

Alice was still looking around the room. "But how do they pay for it? What do people here do to make money?"

"Logging. Or fishing. But it's all for the big companies. Zellerbach Paper takes the logs out on barges. The big canneries take the fish. Some of the Haida have their own small businesses."

The barmaid stopped at their table. She balanced a tray of glasses on the palm of her hand. Some of the glasses were empty, some were full. She began setting down full glasses of beer topped with foam.

Pozzi stopped her with a hand held up: "Honey, I'll pass on the beer. Give me a tomato juice." He patted his round stomach. "My ulcer's acting up." He grinned over at Alice. "Besides, beer's not really my drink."

Alice knew that she was supposed to ask, so she did. "What's your drink?"

"Johnny Walker, Black Label!" Pozzi slapped the table with both hands. "But those days are over. Right, Nathan?"

Nathan turned to Alice. "Would you like a beer?"

She shook her head. "Beer makes my knees feel weak." She looked up at the barmaid. "Could I have a 7-Up?"

The woman gave a quick nod. She was in a hurry. She began picking up the full glasses of beer and setting them back on her tray.

Nathan caught her eye. He held up four fingers. The barmaid set the beer back down for him: one, two, three, four. Four tall, curved glasses of beer, topped with white foam. Nathan reached for his wallet.

"No!" Alice laid her hand on his arm. "Let me pay for something." She dug in the pocket of her jeans. The jeans were tight. She had a hard time digging her fingers in. Her cheeks flushed pink. "Just a minute." She must have gained two pounds since she got here. Pancakes. Biscuits. She drew out a crumpled green wad and opened it up. It was a $10 bill, a U.S. bill. Nathan stared at it. His mouth was tight. There was a wild look in his eyes. Alice had never seen him like this. He had kept his cap on—as if he would be leaving any minute.

But first he raised his glass to her: "Cheers."

He didn't mean it. Alice could see from his eyes that he didn't mean, "Be full of cheer, be happy." Behind his glasses, his eyes were wild and sad.

Under the table, she shifted her foot so that it touched his. But Nathan moved his foot away.

Alice pretended not to notice. She reached for a handful of peanuts from the bowl in front of her. She stuffed them into her mouth.

Pozzi had his arm around Nathan's waist. On the other side, Alice gripped Nathan's arm, to hold him up. They were headed down to the boat, along the plank walkway. Or at least Nathan was. Both Alice and Pozzi were forced to walk in the mud on either side of the narrow plank. Nathan was the only one with clean boots.

Pozzi called over to Alice. "Maybe I should just carry the kid."

Nathan lifted his head. "I'm not a kid."

"You're an ass, is what you are," said Pozzi. "You should have stopped at four beers, not eight."

By the time the boat crossed the inlet to the floathouse, it was dark. In the night sky there was no moon. Only cold stars.

Pozzi shivered. "You can already feel the fall. And it's only July."

Inside, he laid Nathan down on the bed and took his cap off. Nathan's long hair spread out on the bare mattress. Pozzi carefully lifted off the thick glasses. Nathan's was a young face. The skin was pale and smooth above his beard. Pozzi sighed. He felt old enough to be Nathan's father. He *was* old enough!

Pozzi bent to unlace Nathan's boots.

"I'll do that," said Alice.

Pozzi made a fire in the stove. He set water to boil. "Want some coffee?"

"All right." She had covered Nathan with the sleeping bag. Now she sat at the table. The light from the candles made her dark eyes shine.

Pozzi sat down opposite her. He saw those dark, shining eyes. "You're not going to cry on me, are you?"

The girl shook her head.

"You know, it doesn't mean anything, what happened." And he nodded towards Nathan who was passed out on the bed. "The kid's not used to booze. He's no drunk." Pozzi tapped his own chest: "I'm the drunk." He pushed back his chair. He brought two cups back to the table and poured their coffee.

Alice took a sip. She made a face.

"Too strong?" asked Pozzi.

"No, it's all right." She cleared her throat. She spoke carefully. "Nathan has something on his mind." It wasn't a question. But she then looked across at Pozzi, and the question was in her eyes: *What's wrong?*

Pozzi looked away. "Damn," he said, "this coffee hits my stomach hard. I need something to soften the blow."

He searched in the cupboard for a can of cream. He didn't dare tell Alice the truth: that Nathan had downed eight beers because he hated himself. Then she would ask why.

There was no can of cream. Pozzi closed the cupboard. He came back to the table empty-handed. "You asked what's wrong with the kid. I'll tell you. Most people have two sides to them. Hell, maybe animals do too. The Haida thought so. They carved a totem that was part wolf and part fish. They called it a sea-wolf."

Pozzi sipped the black coffee. "Yeah, two sides. And each side fights against the other." He smiled at Alice. "You're like that. I've been watching you. There's a fight going on inside."

Tears shone in the girl's eyes.

Pozzi nodded towards the bed and its sleeper: "Nathan, he's got a fight going on inside of him too. He wants to be wise, a wise old man. And he's just a kid. That's why he likes hanging out with me. I'm old. But I'm not wise." He smiled a sad smile.

Alice blinked, and wiped her cheek. "Why do you have that gold tooth?"

"This?" He touched his front tooth. "This tooth is money in the bank. If I'm ever really broke, I can always sell this tooth for a cup of coffee."

But Alice didn't laugh. And Pozzi wanted to make her laugh—or at least smile. "So, how did you two meet, you and Nathan?"

Alice sighed. "At a party. I wasn't going to go. But then I did, and Nathan was there. He liked me. He didn't seem to mind that I was overweight. Of course I was all dressed up. Not like this—" She looked down at Nathan's baggy shirt, at her jeans.

She kept her head bent. Pozzi watched a tear drop from her eye onto the table. Another tear plopped into her coffee cup. Pozzi felt a laugh rising in his throat. He felt happy for the first time in a long time. Here he was, sitting across from a beautiful young woman.

He forgot about his stomach and its ulcer. He tried to keep a straight face. He fought a smile.

"Why are you smiling?" asked Alice. She sniffed.

Because you're so beautiful. That's what he wanted to say. Instead, he said, "Why do you think you're fat?"

" 'Overweight' was what I said."

"All right. Why do you think that you're overweight?"

"Because I am! Whenever I'm alone, I eat. I can't stop. I just keep eating. It's horrible!"

"But you were alone today…"

"Yes, I was alone. I waited and waited for you guys to come back. Finally I ate 10 biscuits!" She lowered her voice, and hissed, "I hate myself."

Pozzi rolled a cigarette. His fingers moved slowly. "You don't know what it is to truly hate yourself, Alice. Have you ever swallowed down a bottle of mouthwash? Because you had no money for whiskey? Have you?"

"No, of course not," she sniffed.

"Have you ever been so drunk that you passed out on the sidewalk? People just walk around you. Finally you wake up. And the sidewalk is right under your nose, an inch away. And you don't remember how you got there."

Alice wiped both eyes. "Stop talking like that."

Pozzi leaned closer across the table. "Alice, two months ago, that's how I woke up. On the sidewalk. Right under my nose was a cigarette butt. And it wasn't even mine. That's how low I got."

"You're scaring me, Pozzi. You're acting like a different person."

Pozzi jerked back in his chair. "Hey—I'm sorry. Damn. You must think I'm a nut." He shook his head, he shook away that past life.

Alice was staring down into her cup, holding it with both hands. The fire crackled in the stove. The floathouse rocked gently. In the silence, Pozzi could hear Nathan breathe as he rocked in sleep, drawing in rasps of air.

Alice spoke in a quiet voice. "Nathan was cruel to me today. And I don't know why."

"Yeah. He's been a little hard on you."

Alice lifted her face to the candlelight. "I was so excited about the dolphins—I mean, killer whales. Nothing like that has ever happened to me before." Her eyes shone. "They were wild beings, and they spoke to me." Her voice was firm and sure. "They rose up out of the water and spoke to me."

Pozzi couldn't take his eyes off her face. But she was waiting for him to say something.

"I believe you, I do! But Alice, they came up for air. You must know that."

"But that doesn't mean…"

"No, that doesn't mean they didn't speak to you. By the way, killer whales are from the same family as dolphins, so you weren't too far wrong."

"It's strange that they're called killer whales. They seemed so kind."

"Some people call them the sharks of the north."

"But they seemed so gentle in spirit."

"Maybe they weren't hungry. Maybe they'd just eaten a seal or two. But tell me."

"Tell you what?"

"Tell me what you saw."

"Really? You want to hear? Well, I was just lying there, right outside." Alice pointed. "I felt very alone, but I wasn't scared. Well, maybe a little. You see, I've never been out of the city before. But at that moment I felt strangely calm. And that's when it happened. I was looking across at the forest. My head was almost level with the water. And something black and shiny broke the surface. I felt a warm mist over my face.

"That's when they blew. That was their old air, pushed out of their blowholes."

"It was?" Alice cupped her cheeks with her hands. "It felt like a blessing… that warm mist. It tasted salty." She shook her head in wonder. "It's the strangest thing when something like that happens to you. You can't believe it. I *still* can't believe it. But at the time, I felt like a changed person. I felt sure that everything was going to be different, for ever after."

"But then you went and ate 10 biscuits."

Alice laughed. "No, not 10. It was more like 15. I had to cook up another whole pan of them. But that was later, after I'd waited and waited for you guys to come back."

"Nothing lasts. Not even a blessing from the Pope. We think we've changed, but we haven't."

"*You* have. Tonight, at the pub, you only drank tomato juice."

"Yeah. Tomato juice." Pozzi poked out his cigarette on a plate. Alice was staring at the flame of a candle. Pozzi could see that she was still thinking about the killer whales. He ran a hand back over his hair, over his bald spot. "You know, Alice, this might be the only time we get to talk. Like this."

"You mean, alone, without Nathan?"

"Yeah. So I just want to say…"

There was a loud bang as Nathan flung his arm against the wall. He was still asleep, dreaming.

"Don't worry about the kid. He'll be fine in the morning."

Nathan moaned in his dream.

Alice rose from her chair. She went to him. She drew back the sleeping bag. Then she turned to Pozzi. "Can you blow out the candles?"

"Sure. Sure."

The candles sizzled. Their smoke filled the darkness. Pozzi lay down on his narrow bed.

His bed was by the door. Air blew through the cracks around the door and cooled his face. He needed to cool down. Think of Grace, he told himself. But all he could think of was Alice. And the fact that she lay just across the room.

Grace was nothing like this girl. Grace was hard. She'd had a hard life. She was a bartender. That was how they'd met: Grace behind the bar, and Pozzi climbing onto a bar stool.

Lying in the dark, he licked his lips. He could sure use a drink. None of that watery beer. What he needed was something stronger. But he should keep his mind from wandering in that direction.

His mind wandered towards Alice again. Was she still awake? He didn't want to make a fool of himself. His head lifted from the mattress. "Alice?"

"Yes?"

"You all right?"

"Yes."

"Well, good night."

"Good night, Pozzi."

He lay back. He needed a cigarette.

But whenever he lit up a cigarette, he thought of Grace. And her cough. And the cancer. He was going to marry Grace. As soon as he got back to Seattle. Just the thought of it made him sweat. But maybe they wouldn't fight so much if they were married.

He turned on his side. He pulled the blanket up to his neck. As he slept, he dreamed of Alice. He dreamed that she had crossed the room, and was standing by his bed.

*T*he whaleboat is being tossed about by high waves. The sea is angry. Scowling Frog is angry. The two men in the boat are yelling at each other. Scowling Frog can hear them. These are the thieves who have stolen him away from his village. They don't realize what they have done. They don't know that he was carved as a memorial pole, for a Haida drowned at sea. And now, one of these two men must drown.

4

COLD FIRE

At the bellow of a horn, Nathan leapt out of bed as if shot. He stood there, holding his head in his hands. The floathouse rocked from side to side. Nathan rocked with it, as if still drunk. His head ached. His mouth tasted awful. He had slept in his baggy clothes.

The horn blasted again—a long, deep blast. The sound was so loud that it shook the floor of the floathouse. Nathan opened his eyes. It was daylight.

"What time is it, Pozzi? Where's my glasses?"

"They're right here," said Alice.

Nathan opened the door.

The tugboat loomed beyond the dock. It blocked any other view. The seagoing tug was 100 feet long. High on its deck, a man leaned on the railing. It was the tug's captain. Nathan had first met him a week ago. The man's face wore a cheerful grin. "Good morning. Did I wake you?"

Nathan nodded. The swell from the tug's arrival still rocked the dock under his feet. He fought to keep his balance. The captain called down again: "Well, Sonny? Can you be ready in 15 minutes?"

Nathan woke up. He squatted down on the edge of the dock and splashed cold water over his face. The saltwater stung his eyes. He stood up. "Yes sir. We'll be ready." He limped back inside.

Pozzi was still sitting on his bed in his underwear. His pocket-watch lay open in his hand. He stared at it. "It's six o'clock. Do I have time to shave?"

"No! Get packed. Alice, roll up the sleeping bag."

Nathan packed what food was left into his knapsack. He laid his hand on the stove: cold. He looked around the room. "Alice! What's the matter? You're still lying in bed!"

"Where are we going?"

"Back to Seattle."

"I don't want to go back to Seattle." She lay on her back, with her arms on top of the sleeping bag. Her long arms were bare and pale.

Nathan sat down on the edge of the bed. Into her open hand he slipped his finger. Her own fingers closed around it. She turned her head and looked out the window towards the shore. Nathan followed her gaze. The green darkness of the forest drew back into itself.

"I want to stay here," Alice said. "In this little house. I want to wait here for the killer whales to come back. They know I'm here. One of them looked at me. He looked right into me. He knew me right away, who I really am." She turned her face back to Nathan. "And you don't." She let go of his finger.

"Alice, *please*. Just get up, get dressed."

"But why do we have to go now? Can't we stay a few more days?"

"Alice, the tug is here *now*. And the captain is willing to give us a tow as far as Port Hardy. It's not even legal. He's doing us a favour."

"But won't he be back again?"

"Not for another week. He has to continue on down to Vancouver."

"And then he turns around and comes back?"

"Yes."

"Well, let's go then—in a week."

"Alice, for god's sake! I have no money left for food or gas. I *have* to go back."

"And you won't take any money from me. No, of course not. All right—go." Alice sat up in bed. "Pozzi and I will stay here." She held the sleeping bag against her chest. "Will you stay here, Pozzi?"

The man was pulling on his shirt. He stopped.

Alice pushed her leg against Nathan, pushing him off the bed. "You go. Pozzi and I will stay here until the tugboat comes back." She looked over at Pozzi. "They'll give us a ride, won't they?"

He could only nod. His arm was still halfway in its sleeve.

"Pozzi!" Nathan turned on him. "What the hell is going on? You know I can't pull this off without you."

Pozzi shrugged his shoulders. "What? What did I say?"

Nathan picked up a plastic jug. "I'm going to get drinking water." He stomped out, leaving the door open. Out on the dock he could still hear Pozzi's loud voice: "Damn it, Alice, you put me in a spot. It was a nice spot, don't get me wrong. But I can't let Nathan go alone."

"Why not? He won't even have to steer the boat. He can *sleep* the whole way."

"No, you don't understand. You don't know the Hecate Strait…"

Nathan ran limping along the dock to the shore, to get water from the creek. He returned carrying the heavy jug, limping along as fast as he could.

At the high deck of the tugboat, a woman leaned at the rail. She called down to Nathan: "You having woman trouble, honey?" The captain joined the woman. "This here is my wife. She came along for the trip." He put his arm around her, and laughed. "Sonny," he called down, "never take a woman on a boat. It's bad luck."

The crew of the tug was busy on the deck. One of the men waved at Nathan below, and pointed to the whaleboat: "That's an old-timer you got there. How's it run?"

"Great." Nathan pointed to the large engine box in the middle of the whaleboat. "It's got a 1928 Star engine."

The captain was leaning over the rail. "Come alongside, Sonny. I got a towrope for you."

Nathan yelled for Pozzi.

"Coming!"

By the time Pozzi came out, Nathan was already in the whaleboat. The engine was running. There was only one rope left to untie. Pozzi had his arms full. He carried Nathan's pack, and his own, and Alice's suitcase. He dumped it all into the boat and climbed in. He began untying the last rope.

"Where is she?" asked Nathan.

But here came Alice. She carried the sleeping bag in her arms. Her hair was uncombed. Her eyes were red from weeping. Pozzi helped her into the boat, at the bow. She stayed there, sitting on the foredeck, in front of the engine. She clutched the sleeping bag on her lap. The bag was still puffy and full. She hadn't rolled it up yet. It seemed to give her comfort, to hold it.

Nathan tried to keep his voice light. "Alice, we need your weight back here."

Pozzi leaned toward Nathan. "I don't think that's the right approach. Let her stay there for now. She needs time to pout."

The rope that the captain lowered down was a thick coil of yellow plastic. "Tie it on the ring behind the barge. Use the full length of the rope. You'll need it."

"Yes sir." The rope was heavy, almost two inches thick.

"Remember, you're on your own. I'm not responsible for anything that happens out there. I'd be fired if the company ever heard that I gave some kid a tow."

"Yes sir."

"You've got five minutes. I want to catch the tide."

"Yes sir."

"Good luck."

"Thank you, sir."

Pozzi muttered under his breath. "You'd think this was the goddamn Navy."

Nathan pretended not to hear. He steered the whaleboat towards the rear of the tug, and on past it. Along the shoreline to the left, the forest was still green. But higher on the slope the trees faded into fog.

A huge barge of logs loomed in the distance.

Nathan followed the towrope that lay slack on the water. It stretched back at least 300 feet to the log barge. As they approached the barge, he steered around it. The logs rose as tall as a house. Cables held them in place.

The piled logs were shaggy with bark. The smell of cedar and fir was in the air. The whaleboat chugged past, under the looming load, then circled around behind it. And there, at the back of the barge, was the iron ring.

"Alice, can we trade places?" Pozzi stood up in the middle of the boat. He held one end of the towrope. Alice was still sitting on the foredeck, with the sleeping bag in her arms.

Nathan called to her, "Come back here, sit by me." His voice was gentle.

She lifted her red eyes and looked at him.

"Please," he added. There was already too much weight in the front, from the totems. They lay right at Alice's feet, right under where she sat. "Come on," he said, "I'll help you roll up the sleeping bag." Nathan held his breath. But she didn't step on the totems. Instead, she stepped over the canvas with care.

She climbed around the engine box. Pozzi went forward on the other side. At the bow he climbed onto the foredeck with the rope. "This damn thing weighs a ton."

"Tie it well," called Nathan. "That's our lifeline."

Pozzi tied one end of the rope to the iron ring, and the other end to the whaleboat's bow. Nathan put the engine into reverse, and the boat pulled backwards, away from the barge of logs. Soon the barge was far ahead of them, and the yellow rope stretched tight across the water.

Pozzi cupped his hands around his mouth. "Ready!" he shouted from the foredeck. He paused, and then yelled even louder. "ALL CLEAR!"

The tug answered from far ahead. Its horn gave a short blast. The mountains took the sound, and rolled it back and forth, from shore to shore.

Alice chose to sit by herself, not by Nathan. She sat to one side of the bench that stretched behind the engine. An engine now silent. Alice faced forward, leaning against the rolled-up sleeping bag. She trailed her hand over the side of the boat. Her fingers didn't quite reach the water.

The water was flat and grey. Under the whaleboat it slid past in silence. The forest slid past also. It was leaving her. The floathouse came into view. It slowly slipped by, empty. She had remembered to close its door. The little cove cupped the floathouse, and held it like a memory. That first night, she had held Nathan in her arms, in that little house. His head had lain heavy on her shoulder. And she had said to herself: *This is my man, this is my future.*

The floathouse was now behind them. The shoreline curved in and out as the whaleboat passed. They were being towed eastward through the inlet. There was no jerk in the line. The pull from ahead was steady. The tugboat was somewhere far in front of the barge.

Within the hour, they passed Sandspit and the airport. The whaleboat passed out of Skidegate Inlet, into the open sea. Looking south, the grey water and the grey sky blurred together. There was no line between them.

"I'm ready for breakfast. What about you two?"

It was Nathan who had spoken—for the first time since they'd left the cove. Alice turned her head slightly. She could see Nathan out of the corner of her eye. He leaned with his back against the stern. His arms were folded across his chest. No need to steer. The tiller wavered as the boat was pulled through the water.

Alice turned back to the sea. She shivered. She needed Nathan's jacket. And she was hungry.

"Alice?" Nathan touched her shoulder.

In a moment, she felt the weight of his jacket over her back. She pulled it around her. The wonderful smell of it.

She listened to the hiss of the water beneath the whaleboat. Far ahead, the tugboat's horn sounded. "OOO-GAH." The deep bellow rolled through the mist. The sound was quickly swallowed by the fog. Alice felt the mist on her face. She opened her mouth, and tasted the salty mist on her tongue.

"Breakfast is served," said Nathan.

Alice turned. "Oh," she smiled. Laid out on the bench was a tin of sardines and a loaf of bread.

"Pozzi, pass me the jug of water." Nathan lifted the jug in the air: "To calm waters ahead." He took a long swig from the jug. Then he passed it on to Alice.

The water was cold and fresh in her mouth. It was creek water, from the beach at the cove. Her spirits lifted. She accepted a slice of bread from Nathan.

"Wait." He laid a sardine across her slice.

The sardine had no head or tail. It was just a small, oily body. Alice folded the slice of bread over the little fish, wrapping it in a blanket. She ate three of these, and drank more water. It was like a party. They sat in a circle. Nathan was at the stern. Pozzi and Alice sat at opposite ends of the bench, with the food between them. There was no engine noise, no need to raise their voices to be heard.

"I have a surprise." Alice reached under the bench for her small suitcase. "I have some cookies in here." The box of cookies was only half full. She had eaten the other half the day before. After the 15 biscuits.

They passed the box around the circle. They leaned back against the sides of the boat. They made more toasts with the water jug. To health. To wealth.

Then Nathan began a song about life on the sea in sailing ships. His voice was strong and deep. Alice had heard him sing this before. Now, with her face lifted to the mist, she listened once again. The mist felt so fresh on her skin. She closed her eyes.

They were happy, each of them. Alice knew why she was happy: Nathan was being kind. He was looking at her with shining eyes. Like the night when they first met, in Seattle.

Pozzi stared across at Alice. He was happy just to look at her. She was leaning back against the side of the boat. Her head was tipped back and her eyes were closed. Pozzi could see that her hair was uncombed. And no more blue dress. She wore jeans that were dirty with soot and grease, and Nathan's big red and black shirt. But to Pozzi she looked wonderful.

Nathan was still singing in his deep, strong voice. But the fog was thicker now, it muffled the sound. As he ended the song, Nathan leaned forward. "Kiss," he said to Alice. Pozzi looked away. He rubbed his cheeks. He needed a shave.

Pozzi got out his shaving kit. He dipped his shaving brush over the side, into the water. Then he soaped his face.

"Don't you need a mirror to do that?" asked Alice. She was watching him draw the razor over his chin. Pozzi dipped the razor overboard. "Nope." He started shaving his upper lip. "I just pretend that I'm looking into a mirror."

He cleaned the razor in the water once more. "You want to borrow this, Nathan? You can shave off that ugly thing on your face."

Nathan smiled. He lifted his chin and ran his fingers through his beard. Then he took off his cap with the long ribbons. By now, Alice was combing her hair. Nathan waited for her to finish. "May

I use that?" After he'd combed his long hair, he handed the comb over to Pozzi.

Pozzi held the comb up for Alice to see: "Do you mind?"

Nathan laughed. "Hey! We're all in the same boat! Of course she doesn't mind."

Alice smiled and shook her head. No, she didn't mind. Pozzi could see that she still wore that kiss on her lips. He fingered the comb. He ran it back through his thinning hair. His stomach was beginning to hurt again.

The fog soon closed in. Looking ahead, Pozzi could no longer see the barge. The line of yellow rope ended just ahead of the bow, and faded into fog. The thick mist was all around them. He dug in his knapsack for his woolen cap. He pulled it down over his ears.

The fog drifted between them in the boat. Alice's face was blurred in the mist. Far off, the tug's deep horn sounded once again. When Alice spoke, Pozzi had to lean forward to catch her words.

"I said, have we turned south yet, towards Seattle?"

"No. Not yet. First we cross Hecate Strait."

"That's the bad place you talked about. When do we get there—to Hecate Strait?"

"We're on it."

"Now?"

"Now. And we're very lucky. The Strait is being a pussycat today."

Alice's voice seemed to come from far away. "Are we safe?"

"Hell no. No one is ever safe. Life isn't safe."

Nathan spoke up. "Alice, nothing is going to happen. We're headed due east. We'll be across the Strait by nightfall. The tug will turn south when we reach the mainland."

"And where the tug goes, we follow," added Pozzi. The words came from his mouth, but he couldn't see who he was talking to. Alice and Nathan were sitting no more than four feet away from him. But for moments at a time, he lost them to the fog. And was lost himself. He felt like a ghost.

The tug's horn sounded its warning again. Another horn answered. A chill ran down Pozzi's spine. He knew the danger they were in. The tugboat and all of the big fishing boats had radar. With radar they had eyes to see through the fog. But the whaleboat rode too low on the water to show up on any radar screen. In this fog, the whaleboat itself was a ghost. A fishing boat could loom out of the fog at any moment. *Curse Nathan!* This was all his idea. He'd wanted to catch a free ride.

Another horn sounded, from a great distance. At least Pozzi *hoped* that it was from a great distance. The fog played tricks with sound. He wiped his face of sweat. But it wasn't sweat. It was the mist, the fog. Pozzi let his mind drift. What if he and Alice had stayed behind? At this moment the two of them could be sitting in the floathouse, playing cards. There would be a fire in the wood stove. The room would be warm. The fog would be outside—a white mist at the windows. There would be just the two of them…

But he must not think that way. Grace was the woman for him, not Alice. Alice was young, Grace was his own age. She knew him for what he was. And he knew Grace for what she was: a hard-faced woman. But she loved him. That was what mattered. Right?

Yet his mind drifted to Alice.

The mist parted. Both Alice and Nathan were looking at him. Pozzi's cheeks grew hot. Did they know what he'd been thinking?

Something on the bottom of the boat caught Nathan's eye. He leaned over and picked up a clump of mud. "What's this? And here's some more." He frowned. He was always after Pozzi to keep the boat tidy. "Where did all this mud come from?"

Alice and Pozzi were sitting across from each other. Their eyes met. Alice started to laugh, and Pozzi joined in. Soon they were laughing so hard that they couldn't stop.

Nathan had to shout them down. "All right! Who tracked mud into this boat. It sure in hell wasn't me."

Pozzi tried to stop laughing. "Nathan, I give up. It was me."

"And me," Alice gasped.

Still laughing, Pozzi explained. "The mud is from our visit to the pub. We had to almost carry you down to the boat. You were too drunk to walk on your own."

"Oh."

Nathan bent to scoop up more clumps of mud. He threw them over his shoulder into the sea. He was sitting on the high bench at the stern, so he was looking down on Alice and Pozzi. But he must be feeling very small. Pozzi grinned at him. "You don't remember that night, do you."

"No, I don't." Nathan wiped his hands on his pants. "I guess I'm a jackass."

"You could say that." Pozzi winked at Alice. Then he looked about. The mist had drawn back a bit. But the horn of the tugboat still sounded, every few minutes. One long blast, then two short blasts. He pulled out his watch: it was past noon. "This fog won't burn off. We'll be fogged in all day."

"And tonight?" Alice asked Pozzi.

"Tonight, Alice, there will be stars."

"How can you be sure?"

"I can't. But things are bound to change. Hecate Strait is a very moody body of water." He glanced over at Nathan. "Just like some people. Moody."

"But you think there will be stars?" said Alice. "Maybe you're one of those people who can feel the weather in their bones. You must have been a sailor once. I bet that you were in the Coast Guard or something. I bet you've sailed all over."

"Before this, the only sailing that I've done was in the Seattle Library. And Nathan has a book on tying knots. I read that twice. There was nothing else to read in the floathouse." Pozzi looked at Nathan. "I was told I could only bring two books along on this trip. The kid here wanted me to travel light."

Alice's face was lost to him for a moment. But her voice came through the mist: "You don't seem like the kind of person who would love books."

He talked to her ghost. "Honey, I read at every chance I can get. I used to read in my taxicab all the time. If I didn't have a fare, I'd park under a streetlight and open up a book. Kept me out of trouble."

"I'd be happy to do that for you." Nathan took the can of baked beans from Alice. He pulled out his knife from his pocket. It was a Swiss Army knife. It had a corkscrew, even a small scissors. And a can opener.

Nathan set the opened can of beans onto the bench between Alice and Pozzi. There was no worry that the can might slide off. The sea was still calm and flat. Not a wave, not a ripple. And no fog.

At the bow, the yellow rope pulled taut. The barge could now be seen far ahead. It was a huge, dark shape in a darkening sky. The whaleboat had parted the curtain of fog, only to enter the evening.

Nathan opened the second can of beans. He worked his red knife around the top of the tin. They had made it. They had safely crossed Hecate Strait. Already the tugboat had swung a wide curve, and was now headed south. They were now being towed down the Inland Passage.

He handed the can of beans over to Pozzi. Alice was still digging in Nathan's pack. "I can only find one spoon."

"Give it to Pozzi," said Nathan. And he opened out a tiny spoon on his Swiss Army knife. He handed the knife to Alice. "You first."

Alice made a show of it. She crooked her little finger, and ate in dainty bites. But then she pointed to the sky. "Umm!" Her mouth was full of beans. She swallowed. "Star light, star bright. First star I see tonight…" She was pointing at the evening star.

Indeed, the sky was soon filled with stars. Pozzi had been right, the weather had changed. The stars blinked and sparkled in the blackness overhead. The mainland was now only a dark line of mountains to the east.

Pozzi's voice broke through the stillness. "Is there anything else to munch on?"

Alice spoke up. "I have a candy bar in my suitcase."

Pozzi laughed. "What *else* have you got in that suitcase?"

"Nothing else, I swear. Just clothes."

"Well, we might have to eat those too. Nathan believes in keeping his crew hungry."

Nathan kept quiet. Back in Seattle, he'd agreed to pay for the whole trip—for the boat and the food and the gas. All that Pozzi would have to bring was his knowledge of the Northwest Coast. Pozzi had held up his end of the deal. But Nathan was now broke. And there was only flour and oatmeal left to eat.

But nothing could spoil Nathan's present happiness. The tugboat would be towing them through the long night. The Inland Passage was a safe route. The islands to the west would protect them from the open sea.

The whaleboat had no running lights, not when the engine was shut off. But Nathan could see Alice by the faint light of the stars.

He spoke quietly. "Alice, look behind us, look at our wake."

Their wake streamed behind them in the darkness. It glowed with a blue-green light. Nathan lifted an oar over the side, and held it out behind them. The oar cut with water with a blue-green fire. Every ripple and wave glittered.

"It's tiny algae," said Nathan.

"It's magic," said Pozzi.

Alice said nothing. She only stared at their glittering wake. Even after Nathan had lifted the oar from the water, she stared behind them. "It's magic," she whispered.

Nathan yawned, loudly. The yawn was to show Pozzi how tired he was. "Can you take the first shift, Pozzi? I need a few hours sleep." He turned to Alice. "Come on." He made his way forward. In front of the engine box there was just enough space for two people to lie down. It was dry. "Bring the sleeping bag," he called to Alice.

He spread the bag over the bottom of the boat. They lay down together, facing each other. Nathan looked into her shadowed eyes. "I'm sorry."

Alice lay silent.

Nathan pulled her closer. "I'm sorry I got so drunk. I've never done that before. I'm sorry."

"And you're sorry that you let me come along."

"No, that's not true."

"I shouldn't have nagged you to let me come."

"No, no—I'm glad that you're here."

They spoke in whispers.

"Are you warm enough?"

"Yes. Are you?"

"Mmm. Do you think you can sleep?"

"If you can. But first I want to see your face."

"Wait." Nathan reached into his pants pocket. "I brought a candle from the floathouse." It was only a stub. He struck a match, and lit a flame. "We need something to hold the candle—the tin can from the beans."

"I'll go get it." Alice started to rise.

"No, let me." Nathan crawled towards the back of the boat. Pozzi was sitting at the stern, smoking. The boat's wake glittered behind him on the black water. The tip of Pozzi's cigarette glowed bright red as he pulled the smoke into his lungs.

"Wake me in four hours, Pozzi," Nathan whispered.

"Whatever you say, kid."

Seagulls ride the wind. Above the high waves they swoop and circle. The crash of waves poses no danger to them. The wind is their playmate. The gulls take delight in its force. They are at home in the wind and waves that bring danger to men.

As the gulls circle, the whaleboat is far below. The boat is so small in the wide sea. It is being tossed about by huge waves. It is like a toy boat. It is the sea's plaything.

5

THE YELLOW ROPE

The morning brought no sun. The sky hung heavy and grey. The sea was an ugly grey-green. The whaleboat was still being towed south behind the barge. But their free ride was no longer so smooth. A heavy swell lifted the boat.

Nathan sat on the high bench at the stern. He kept one hand on the tiller. He did this out of habit. He had little control of the boat. The yellow rope that pulled them had all the control.

Nathan poked Pozzi with the tip of his boot. "Pozzi, wake up."

The sleeping man lay crosswise on the bottom of the boat. His knees were drawn up. He snored. His wool cap was pulled down over his eyes.

Alice was still asleep up at the front. But she wouldn't be asleep much longer. The water was getting rough. They had left the safety of the Inland Passage. It was now an open sea to the west.

Nathan poked Pozzi again. He needed the map from his pack.

And Pozzi was using Nathan's pack for a pillow. Finally, Nathan pulled the bag out from under him.

Pozzi's head fell with a thud. "What the hell!" He sat up. The wool cap was still over his eyes.

Nathan opened the map across his lap. He checked his compass.

Pozzi pushed his cap off his eyes. He lifted himself onto the middle bench, and blinked. "Where are we?"

Nathan pointed to the coast of the mainland. "I think we're coming up on Cape Caution."

Pozzi squinted towards the southeast. "I don't see anything. Oh, yeah, I see it now. So how far are we from Port Hardy?"

Nathan handed the map to Pozzi. He put his hand back on the tiller. Again, it was only from habit. Out of habit, he began steering the nose of the boat into the waves. It gave him something to do. He had been awake and on watch since 3:00 a.m. He had seen the dawn break. The black of the night had turned to a grey morning.

The waves were now higher. The whaleboat rode the long swells. A cold breeze was blowing from the west across the water.

"This map says that we're on Smith Sound." Pozzi looked up from the map. "Is that bad? Are we in trouble?"

"Not yet." Nathan was truly steering now, as each wave rose out of the sea. The wind grew stronger. It was now blowing from the west *and* from the east. Nathan had to raise his voice to be heard: "You can see on the map where we're headed. Queen Charlotte Strait. It's between the mainland and Vancouver Island. The entrance to the Strait can be rough. The tides fight each other. And this wind won't help."

White foam now crested the waves. The map flapped in Pozzi's hands. He folded it up, fighting with the wind. "I don't remember coming up this way."

"Well, we did. You must have been asleep. But it wasn't so bad on the trip up. Not like this."

"Will it get worse?" asked Pozzi at the top of his voice.

"Will it, Nathan?" Alice was crawling towards him. She held on to the side of the boat as she crawled around the engine box. Her hair blew across her face. "What's going on? I was dreaming. I heard you guys talking, and your words were strange." She rubbed at her eyes, to wake up. "Each word had two meanings. It was a terrible dream." She turned and looked out over the waves. "It's so strange. There's all this water around us. But we can't drink it. Pozzi, can you hand me the jug?"

She took a long swallow. Then she passed the jug to Nathan.

He held the jug in one hand and tipped it up. One hand was still on the tiller as he closed his eyes. The cool creek water ran down his throat. The boat pitched backwards. He felt fear in his belly. It was only a flutter of fear. A voice spoke in his head. It was his father's voice: *This is all your fault.*

Nathan's eyes were closed for only a moment. When he opened them, the whaleboat was being pulled sideways into a wave. The wave broke against them. The splash of spray hit Pozzi in the back of the neck. "Hey! You trying to drown me?"

"Nathan?" It was Alice. She now sat at his feet, in the bottom of the boat. He hoped that his fear didn't show on his face.

"What can I do to help?" she cried.

"Nothing yet. Just stay where you are, you're fine there." And safer. Nathan's seat was almost level with the rim of the boat. It gave him a view of what was ahead. But he could feel the sea at his back. His grip tightened on the handle of the tiller. The boat dipped into a valley. And then the next wave rose in front of them. He steered into it. The wave lifted the bow of the boat, passing under as they rode its crest. Spray hit Nathan's face. The taste of the sea was on his lips. His fear lifted to excitement.

Pozzi raised his voice against the wind. "My stomach is giving me trouble."

"Then eat something," Nathan yelled back at him. "Look in my pack."

There was a last can of beans. Pozzi opened them with Nathan's knife. Nathan shook his head, no he didn't want any. And Alice made a face. So Pozzi ate the can of beans himself.

Alice yelled against the wind, "What's the name of that place we're going?"

"Port Hardy."

Alice turned to face Pozzi. "When we get to Port Hardy, I'll buy all of us breakfast."

Nathan broke in: "It might not be breakfast. I doubt that we'll get there before lunch." If we're lucky, he could have added.

"All right, I'll buy lunch. What will you order, Pozzi?"

"Me?" He didn't look too good.

"Yes. And I'm paying. So order anything you want."

Pozzi rubbed his chin. "I need a shave." The boat pitched and rolled. Pozzi grabbed the bench.

"Hurry up!" yelled Alice, "I'm hungry."

"All right. I'll have steak and onions."

"What about a salad?"

"I never eat anything that's green."

They were both shouting.

"What about dessert?"

"I don't like sweets."

Alice turned to Nathan. She forced a smile. She was holding on to the edge of his seat. "What about you? What will you order? I have lots of Canadian money left in my purse. I have to use it up."

But Nathan wasn't listening anymore.

"Pozzi, I think you better start the engine. We need to get more slack in the towrope." Nathan kept his eyes to the front. The sea was coming at them with more force. The waves rose higher. The next one lifted the bow until the whole boat tipped back, rising… then tipped forward as it rode down the wave's steep back.

Pozzi yelled above the wind. "It won't start! The engine won't fire!"

"Keep trying!" Nathan pulled his cap down low over his brow. The cap's long ribbons flew behind him in the wind.

"This is crazy," yelled Pozzi. "Why doesn't that captain head for shore?"

"He can't! It's too rough. And he can't risk losing his barge of logs."

The next wave lifted them. They could see the barge far ahead. The huge barge rolled from side to side. It was taking the full blow of each wave. Nathan knew that if those logs broke loose, they would head straight back at the whaleboat.

"Try the engine again!" He turned to Alice. "Get the life jackets under the foredeck. Put one on." Nathan's glasses were blurred with spray. He wiped his sleeve across them. He watched as Alice crawled past Pozzi. She crawled around the engine box. Pozzi had the lid up. He was shaking his head.

A tall wave loomed in front of them. They rode it up, up. The towrope pulled them through the crest of the wave. Water spilled over the bow. They rode down the wave's steep back. The yellow rope went slack for a moment. The whaleboat seemed to hold still. It rested in the bottom of a valley. The valley was walled with waves. Then waves from left and right crashed upon them, splashing into the boat. And once more, the yellow rope jerked them forward, to the next wave, and the next.

Here came Alice, crawling back to him. Her hair hung wet around her face. She was soaked. But she wore a life jacket. "There's only two!" she screamed. She dragged the other life jacket behind her. "Take it!" She held it up to him. Nathan shook his head. He pointed at Pozzi.

"No!" Alice screamed. "Please! You're sitting right on the edge, you could get hit by a wave, you could fall out of the boat!"

Nathan shook his head again. It was more than a matter of pride. He pointed at Pozzi. "He can't swim!"

Nathan could hear his father's voice at his ear. It was a only whisper. But Nathan could hear it under the howl of the wind: *Is this what you call your freedom—the chance to drown yourself and other people?*

"HOO-RAY!" Pozzi lifted his fist into the air. The engine had started.

A wave hit the boat from behind. It splashed up against Nathan's back. His sweater was wet to his skin. But he wasn't cold. He felt nothing. The sea sucked the whaleboat into a hollow at the bottom of a wave. Water poured in from the sides. They were fighting a cross-sea.

"Pozzi, get the bucket! Start bailing."

Pozzi turned on him with a sneer. "*You* get the bucket, damn you!" He was trying to put his arms through the life jacket. His face was pale. Alice was trying to help him. Six inches of water washed back and forth in the bottom of the boat.

Nathan steered into the next wave. The engine was going at full speed. The wave lifted them high.

"Pozzi, untie the towrope! We have to get free."

Pozzi nodded, "Hold your horses!" Alice tightened the straps of the life jacket across his chest.

But up at the bow, Pozzi had trouble. He couldn't untie the tow-rope. The knot was being pulled too tight. The rope was dragging their full weight through the sea.

"Use my knife," yelled Nathan. He passed the knife to Alice, who passed it forward to Pozzi.

"The rope's too thick! It's plastic! She won't cut!"

Then Pozzi tried the ax. He hacked at the knot. The ax bounced off the plastic rope.

"HEY!" Pozzi waved the ax in the air. Nathan also saw the fishing boat, far to the east. It was riding out the storm. All its nets were drawn up, its tall cranes rocking back and forth. "Pozzi, sit down!" Nathan shouted. "They can't help us." And he steered into the next looming wave.

Alice had crawled to get the bucket, and was now bailing out water from the bottom of the boat. But each time she was able to rest, she held to Nathan's ankle. She shouted, "I don't want you to fall overboard." Her hand circled his ankle with a tight grip. It almost hurt, she gripped so tightly. She must think that if she held on to his ankle, she could save him. Maybe she was right.

The whaleboat passed the northern tip of Vancouver Island. The sea was still grey-green, and choppy with waves. But the wind and tides had played out their tricks.

Alice lifted herself up to the bench in the middle of the boat. She pushed her hair back from her forehead. She was wet, from her head down to her sneakers. But there was no longer any water in the bottom of the boat. She had bailed for hours. The boat was now being towed through a calmer sea. But Nathan had kept the engine idling. He was taking no more chances.

Pozzi sat at the other end of the bench. His face was still pale. He had pulled off his wool cap, and his hair stuck out from his head. And he was right: he needed a shave. Alice laughed. "You look terrible." As soon as she said it, she was sorry. She leaned forward. "Are you all right?"

Pozzi nodded. Then he turned on the seat. He leaned over the side of the boat—and was sick.

Alice had to listen, but she didn't have to watch. She lifted her face to the sky. The sun had burned through the greyness. Alice gazed up at a sky that was patched with blue. It was the most beautiful colour. She had forgotten about blue.

"Alice?"

She pretended not to hear Nathan. She kept her face to the sky. She didn't dare look at him. He must think she was crazy. A crazy woman holding on to his ankle all those hours.

The blast of a horn sounded far ahead. It was the tug. Three more short blasts followed. Nathan stood up. He squinted. "I think they're stopping. They must want us to come alongside."

The yellow towrope lay slack on the water. No longer was it pulling the whaleboat. They would soon be under their own power. Nathan steered to the right. "Alice, take the tiller. I'm going to untie the rope."

"I can do it. Let me try." Alice climbed forward. She kneeled on the foredeck. She looked at the knot. The boat rocked on the water. Gulls cried overhead. It was a huge knot. Alice smiled to herself. *If I can untie this knot, then Nathan loves me.* It was a game. She pulled and tugged at the yellow rope. The breeze dried her hair and blew it about. Her fingers were quick and smart, though she broke a nail in the process. *He loves me!*—and she threw the end of the yellow rope into the sea.

Alice was still kneeling on the foredeck when it happened.

Beyond the bow, the sea parted and a warm mist hit her face. It smelled of fish.

The killer whale rose in a burst of spray. Beside it, another blunt head parted the water and shot upwards in a rush. Their twin leap from the water exposed two great glistening backs, and under-bellies of pure white.

"They followed me!" Alice shouted over her shoulder. The killer whales curved toward the water, their tails splashing as they dove.

Alice leaned forward. "Oh, hello, hello!"

And here they came again. Alice held up her hand to stop Nathan. "Don't put the engine in gear yet!"

The killer whales now circled the boat. Alice followed with her eyes. She was down on her hands and knees on the foredeck. She leaned with her face out over the water. *Look at me. Look at me.*

And here he came. His blunt head lifted from the wave. The small black eye at the side of his mouth stared at her for a moment.

And then he was gone.

"It happens all the time," said Pozzi. "A whole pod of killer whales will follow a boat sometimes. Right, Nathan?"

At the tiller, Nathan didn't answer.

And Alice was in her own dream world. Her face glowed. Pozzi stared at her.

The whaleboat was under its own power now. The engine chugged through the choppy sea.

Pozzi went on: "You probably think those killer whales are the same ones you saw before." He was watching her face. "You can't really believe that they followed you all this way."

Pozzi hated himself at that moment. Why was he trying to spoil her happiness? He looked down at his hands. They were shaking. He'd eaten very little food in the last 24 hours. But he knew it wasn't hunger. He was shaking from fear. He reached up and touched his cheek, then looked at his finger. Blood.

When the killer whales had leapt from the sea, Pozzi had been shaving. The razor was at his cheek. And then he'd seen those two fins rise above the rim of the boat. His heart had jumped. His hand had jerked, and he had cut himself.

What had scared him? He'd seen killer whales before. But not this close. Pozzi had seen that single black eye as well. And it hadn't been looking at Alice. It had been looking at *him*. The message was for Pozzi. Something was going to happen to him, and it wouldn't be good.

Pozzi lifted his sleeve to the cut on his cheek. "Alice, I'm sorry."

But Alice was still off in her own world. She held her face up to the sun. Her wet life jacket was steaming in the warmth. Pozzi suddenly felt hot. He pulled at the straps of his own life jacket: he wouldn't need this anymore.

Nathan steered around the barge of logs. They were gaining on the big tug.

Pozzi finished shaving, though his hand still trembled. The sight of those killer whales had filled him with dread. His fear of water, of the sea, had risen in his throat to choke him. Nathan knew nothing of Pozzi's fear. He only knew that Pozzi couldn't swim. He didn't know that Pozzi had almost drowned, as a child.

Pozzi still remembered how it felt to sink from the world, the world of his mother and father… Sinking, falling away from the safe world. His eyes were open underwater. He hadn't tried to draw a breath yet. Deeper and deeper he sank through a blue-green blur. He heard them calling his name, far above at the water's surface…

"Pozzi, will you get out an oar? If we start getting too close to the tug, push us away."

The tug loomed above them. The whaleboat drew alongside. The seagoing tug seemed even bigger than Pozzi remembered.

"Hello, down there." The captain's wife waved from the guard-rail. "We were worried sick about you. But my husband couldn't stop. You can't stop in a sea like that."

Now the captain was at the rail, yelling down. "You're damn fools! And I was a damn fool to give you a tow." His wife patted his arm. He pushed her hand off. "Well, I'm just glad to see that you're alive."

One of the crew lowered a bucket down to them. The bucket swung back and forth at the end of a rope. Pozzi stood up. He braced his feet apart as the boat rocked under him. The captain called down, "You're on your own now. We're going on to Vancouver. Port Hardy is coming up. Take you about an hour to get there. Good luck."

Pozzi caught the bucket on the third swing. A wonderful smell drifted from the bucket. The crewman called down, "There's some turkey in there." Pozzi set the bucket on the seat. He lifted out the turkey meat, wrapped in a white napkin. And some biscuits, and grapes.

Pozzi looked into the bucket again. What he saw there made him break out in a cold sweat.

At the bottom of the bucket was a bottle of whiskey: Johnny Walker, Black Label.

The wharf at Port Hardy stood on long legs. The low tide lapped around the posts. Tiny sea shells clung to the posts where the tide had left them high and dry.

Nathan steered the whaleboat alongside a low dock. Pozzi climbed out first, and held his hand out to Alice. Nathan was the last to set foot on the dock. It swayed under him. Even the stairs leading up to the wharf swayed under his feet. And when he reached the road, the road swayed, rocking from side to side. As he walked, he looked at the weeds growing along the edge of the road. He looked at the tin cans thrown among the weeds. He watched a newspaper tumble down the road on a breeze. Everything looked beautiful. He felt like singing. He kicked at a pebble, and almost fell.

"Wait up." He grabbed Alice's hand.

They went into the first cafe that they came to. They took a booth near the window.

Nathan scooted in after Alice. The plastic seat cover was smooth and cool under him. Seagulls glided beyond the window, circling over the wharf. Under the table, Nathan searched for Alice's hand.

Pozzi was still standing. He'd placed a few coins on the table. Now he dug in his pockets for more. He brought out a single dime, and laid that on the table. "Does anyone have any change? I need to phone Grace."

In a few minutes he was back. He heaped the coins in a pile on the table, and sat down heavily. He slid across to the window and looked out, silent.

"Well? Was she there? Did you talk to her?"

Pozzi shook his head, "No answer." Then he looked across at Nathan and Alice. "Hey!" He slapped the table with both hands. The ashtray jumped. "We're alive!" Then he looked straight at Nathan. "No thanks to you."

Nathan's smile faded.

"Hey, kid, I'm joking!" Pozzi grinned, his gold tooth shining. He leaned across the table and poked Nathan's shoulder. "You did a hell of a job—for a rich kid."

"I'm going to have a milk shake," said Alice. She held the menu with one hand. "A strawberry milk shake, and a tuna sandwich." She slid the menu to Nathan and said, "Remember, I'm paying, okay?"

"Okay." Nathan's also held the menu with one hand. His other hand was under the table, holding Alice's hand.

He was starving. The turkey had not even touched his hunger. He'd eaten an entire drumstick from the bucket lowered down from the tug. The three of them had devoured everything in that bucket. Of course, the bottle of whiskey had gone straight into his knapsack, out of sight. Out of Pozzi's sight. There was no sense in tempting him.

"I'll have steak and onions, the same as Pozzi." Nathan shut the menu. "How's your ulcer, Pozzi?"

"What ulcer? I've been on a diet. No food." He took a noisy sip of his coffee. "Ahhh." He looked at Nathan. "Where's the tin of tobacco?"

"It's in my knapsack on the boat."

"Damn. What I need with this coffee is a cigarette." He looked down at his cup. Then he looked up. "I'll go get it."

But Nathan was already slipping out from the booth. "I'll go." His first thought had been of the bottle of whiskey in the knapsack.

He headed down the road to the wharf. He was glad for the chance to check on the totems. He didn't like leaving the boat so far away, out of sight.

A breeze carried the fresh sea air. Gulls circled overhead with their cries. His ankle was fine, no more limp. Nathan began to run down the road, the ribbons of his hat flying.

*T*he sea is full of sound. Sound moves quickly through the water, and travels far. Killer whales send out clicks and whistles as they search for food. Their voices travel many miles through the sea. When these sound waves finally strike an object in the water they rebound to their source. They tell the killer whale what is out there, in the sea. His own voice returns to tell him if the object is a salmon, or a seal, or a boy.

The boy is drowning. His arms flail underwater. He is falling from the world.

6

The Kelp Bed

Pozzi sat on the engine box. He couldn't keep still. His heels beat time against the side of the box. He faced the stern, where Nathan was reading a tide table. The chart was spread over Nathan's knees. With one finger he traced down a row of numbers on the chart.

"How can you understand that thing?" asked Pozzi.

Nathan kept his head bent over the chart. "I'm learning. You should too, Pozzi. It's important to understand about the tides."

The whaleboat hugged the east coast of Vancouver Island as they travelled south. The late afternoon sent long shadows of trees across the water. But the shadows fell short of the boat. Pozzi rode in full sunshine. He could feel the throb of the engine under his legs. And he could sense Alice at his back. She, too, sat on the engine box, but faced forward. They sat back to back. Pozzi knew that if he leaned backwards, even a little, they might touch.

At that moment Alice leaned back against him. "Were you scared?" she asked quietly.

It took Pozzi a moment to find his voice. "If you're talking of being tossed about by the sea for six hours—the answer is 'yes.'"

He felt the bones of her spine against him. And he let go a little bit. He leaned back too. They leaned their weight against each other.

"I thought we were going to die," she said. "Did you?"

"No."

It was a while before they spoke again.

"I was scared that Nathan would be washed overboard by a wave," Alice murmured over her shoulder.

"I know."

"And if he *had* fallen overboard, the towrope would have kept on pulling us forward. There was no way we could stop and go back. We would have lost him. Am I right?"

"Yes."

Pozzi felt her shudder. He felt it along his own spine. He wanted her to keep talking. He wanted them to stay just like this, and never move.

But the boat moved them forward. It pushed them forward through time. The shadows of the trees leaned out farther from the shore. The sun was sinking. The afternoon would soon be evening, and this moment would pass. Pozzi wanted it to last forever. He could feel each breath that Alice took. They sat like that for a while, back to back, in silence. Then it struck Pozzi: he knew why Alice was silent. She was thinking about Nathan.

Pozzi felt his heart tighten in his chest. He hissed over his shoulder, "You know, the kid is not the marrying kind."

"Yes. I know."

He heard the sadness in her voice. He could have kicked himself. "What the hell. Maybe you can change his mind."

Alice sat up quickly. "Do you think so?" Pozzi had to catch himself from falling backwards.

"Mmm," Alice stretched her arms into the air. "I feel like a swim."

"That water is colder than it looks."

"Do you think so?"

The whaleboat glided across the shadows. Insects darted over the green surface.

"Pozzi, why can't you swim?"

"Why can't fish fly?" He stared at the water.

When Nathan called out his name, Pozzi jerked in surprise. He'd managed to pretend that he and Alice were alone in the boat. Had Nathan been listening to them, all this time? And what did he just ask?

"Well? Were you able get Grace on the phone?"

Pozzi cleared his throat. "No. Then I thought maybe she was at work, so I called the bar. No luck." Pozzi quickly changed the subject. "So why are we going so slow? We'll never get to Seattle at this rate."

Nathan smiled. "I'm in no hurry."

Pozzi kept at him. "You were in a hell of a hurry before. What's changed?"

"Everything."

Pozzi hated that smile on Nathan's face. "And what's this about tides, why should I know anything about tides?"

Nathan laughed. "Pozzi, if you can't read a tide table, you'll never be a sailor."

"Damn right I'll never be a sailor. This is the last time you'll see my ugly face in a boat... Hey!" Pozzi jumped up. He pointed behind Nathan, pointing at their wake: "We've got a bite!"

The fishing line jerked and jiggled. It was tied to the stern of the boat. They'd put out the line in the early afternoon.

"Let me take it, kid." Pozzi pushed Nathan aside. He kneeled on the seat. He lifted the line, and played it in his fingers. He could feel the strength of the fish at the other end.

Fifty feet away a big salmon leapt from the water. His body flapped in the air. He fought the hook in his mouth. Then he splashed. Now he was swimming back and forth. He jerked the line as he swim. He tried to jerk the hook from his mouth.

The bow of the boat grated onto sand. It was a lovely sound. Pozzi jumped from the boat. He pushed the bow up onto the beach. Alice had jumped out on the other side. "Push, Alice!"

"This place is perfect!" she shouted. "Our own little island." She waded from the water, and ran up onto the beach. She held out her arms, and turned around and around. Pozzi watched her.

She fell to the sand. "I love it here!" Then she stood up. "Come on, Nathan. Let's look around."

"First I need to gut this salmon."

"Yuk!" Alice waved to Pozzi. "Come on, Pozzi, let's walk around the island."

Pozzi quickly finished tying up the boat. He heard Nathan call after him. "Bring back some firewood!"

The little island was sandy and dry. Large stones lay on the ground. The island rose to a mound at its centre. The trees that grew there were thin and small. Pozzi found Alice among them, sitting on a rock.

"Pozzi, get your watch out."

"Whatever you say, Alice."

"Now, I'm going to walk around the island. And you have to time me on your watch." She jumped up. "I want to see how long it takes."

"Don't run!" Pozzi called after her. "You're supposed to walk!" He sat down on Alice's rock. He didn't really want to be alone. He didn't want to be alone with his thoughts. He licked his lips. His mouth was dry. He could hear the sound of the ax. It came from the other side of the island. Nathan was cutting firewood.

Maybe Alice wasn't coming back around. Maybe she would stay on the other side, with Nathan.

Pozzi couldn't sit still. He stood up from the rock, and walked down towards the shore. The beach was scattered with grey pieces of driftwood. They looked like old bones, scattered across the sand.

This little scrub island—with no drinking water, no grass. It was just small enough so that Alice could play house. She could pretend that it was her island. Pozzi kicked at a piece of driftwood. It rolled down the beach, and stopped.

In his heart, Pozzi was glad that Grace hadn't answered the phone.

Alice's voice broke into his thoughts. "How long?" She came walking quickly along the beach. She was out of breath when she reached Pozzi. "How long did I take?"

"Oh. Sorry." Pozzi looked down at the watch in his hand. "I forgot to check the time when you left." The truth was, when Alice had left, his eyes had followed her hips in the tight jeans.

"What time is it now?"

"Seven o'clock." The sun was down, but its light still filled the sky. Pozzi put his watch back into his pocket. "It will be dark in a few hours."

"And in the morning we have to leave." Alice picked up a stick of driftwood. She dragged the stick behind her as she walked down to the water. Pozzi followed without thinking. His steps followed the trail drawn in the sand by her stick. The trail curved, this way and that. When it stopped, he looked up. Alice had waded in, still wearing her sneakers. With the stick she poked at the kelp in the water. A brown knob floated on the surface. She poked the stick under the water plant and lifted it up. Long, flat streamers hung like hair from the knob of kelp. She let it drop, and the brown streamers floated out upon the water.

"Look! There's more. They're everywhere." Alice pointed. Knobs of kelp floated offshore. Their long brown streamers stirred and swayed in the slack water. Again she nudged her stick under a strand of kelp, to lift it up.

"Don't do that." Pozzi grabbed the stick from her hand. He threw the stick far out over the kelp bed. The stick splashed, and then floated.

"Why are you mad?" asked Alice.

"I'm not mad."

She waded to shore. "I'm going back." Her head was down.

"I'm not mad," Pozzi called. When he caught up with Alice, he tried to explain. "I'm just feeling jumpy. That kelp gave me the creeps."

Alice was looking up at the sky. A sliver of moon hung over the water. She smiled. "I could spend the rest of my life here."

"Hold out your arms," he told her. And he bent down. He picked up a piece of driftwood, and placed it in her arms. Then he picked up another piece.

He'd soon loaded her arms with firewood.

"Am I your pack mule?" she asked.

Pozzi grinned. "It's good for a woman to be useful."

"You!" She kicked him in the leg. But she didn't drop the firewood. Pozzi then loaded his own arms full.

But Nathan already had a fire going. From the rise of the hill, Pozzi could look down and see the flames. He could hear them crackle. Sparks lifted into the evening sky.

Nathan squatted by the fire. The light from the flames danced on his glasses. He pointed. "You can put the wood over there," he said.

"Yes, sir," said Pozzi. And he dumped the wood where he stood. Alice came up beside Pozzi. "Where shall I put this firewood?"

"Anywhere," said Nathan. And he smiled at Pozzi, and tossed a handful of sand at his feet.

Then Pozzi saw the tent Nathan had erected. The canvas tent was small. It was meant for two people. And Pozzi knew that those two people were Nathan and Alice.

The canvas was from the boat. It now hung over the low limb of a tree, forming a tent that was open at both ends. The corners of the canvas were held down by stones.

Nathan saw Pozzi staring at the tent. "I put it up there, out of the reach of the tide. It's starting to come in, you can hear it. Listen."

It was a tiny sound: the lapping of water upon the sand.

The only cooking pot was dented. It was blackened with the soot of earlier fires. But it still had a handle. Alice carried the pot down to the water. She filled the pot half full. The salty water would be perfect to cook potatoes in. She looked across the water at the coast of Vancouver Island and its thick woods. It was no farther away than a stone's throw. She was on her own little island.

She walked back up the beach. The sliver of moon was now higher, in a darker sky.

Nathan was piling more wood on the fire. The sparks leapt into the evening like new stars, then died away. Alice set the black pot on a stone. From Nathan's pack she pulled out a roll of toilet paper, a flashlight, and a loaf of bread. She had bought all this and more, back at Port Hardy. But where were the potatoes?

Alice felt around inside the backpack. Her fingers touched glass—smooth and cool. The bottle of whiskey. Instead she pulled out the bag of potatoes she'd bought.

She used Nathan's red knife to peel the potatoes. Her fingers worked quickly. She could sense that Pozzi was watching her.

"You have big hands. Let's see if they're bigger than mine." Pozzi held up his hand, with his fingers spread wide. He was waiting. So Alice reached across and matched her hand against his. Pozzi laughed. "Look at this, Nathan. You've got a big girl here. Our hands are the same size."

Alice waited for the potatoes to boil. She *willed* them to boil. The smell of cooking salmon filled the air. The three of them waited for dinner to be ready. Pozzi did most of the talking. And he kept getting up from the fire and walking off into the darkness. Then he'd turn around, and back he would come, and squat down again. "I'm feeling kind of jumpy." He laughed a hollow laugh. "You think it's a Saturday night tonight?"

"Let's see… I flew in on a Wednesday." Alice counted the days on her fingers. "Wednesday, Thursday, Friday… You're right. It's Saturday." She returned her hand to Nathan's hand. They sat side by side at the fire.

"Yeah. It's gotta be Saturday. I wonder if Grace is working the bar." Pozzi stared down at the fire. "Maybe not."

"Do you still plan to marry her?" asked Nathan.

Pozzi's head popped up. "Marry who?"

"Grace. You said you were going to ask her to marry you."

"What's the matter? You think I might dump her, just when she needs me the most?" He got up from the fire, and paced the darkness. It was as if he wanted to leave. But again he came walking back to the circle of light where Alice and Nathan held hands.

Pozzi sat down. "I'll be sleeping on the other side of the island tonight. I need my privacy." And he laughed that hollow laugh again.

Alice had cleaned the pot. The flames of the fire had died away. The bones of the salmon had burned to ash. But still Pozzi sat by the fire. He was silent now. All three of them watched the red coals. The tent sat waiting up on the beach. Alice tried hard not to look in its direction. Soon she would be inside that tent, with Nathan. She squeezed his hand. They looked at one another.

"Well, I guess I'll be heading off." But Pozzi still sat by the fire. No one spoke. Pozzi sighed. Finally he rose to his feet.

Nathan looked up at him. "Your sleeping bag is still in the boat."

"Oh, yeah. My sleeping bag."

Alice spoke up. "Here, Pozzi, use my flashlight."

Pozzi shook his head. "Don't worry about me."

Alice and Nathan waited by the fire.

"Is he getting his sleeping bag?"

"I can't tell."

"Good night, Pozzi," Alice called.

No answer. A limb cracked as he made his way over the little hill, through the thin stand of trees. She started to get up. Nathan pulled her down, "Wait. He's only going to come back again."

So they waited. Alice sat facing the coals of the fire. Nathan's arms were around her, from behind. "Maybe we should put out the fire," she said. "Maybe we should pour water over it."

"Don't worry about it."

"But I *do*."

"Alice."

She turned her head around for the kiss that she knew was coming.

They crawled into the makeshift tent. The canvas hung over the limb of a small tree that was holding very still. There was no wind, not even a breeze. Through the open end of the tent, Alice could see the stars. She lay on her back. Nathan lay beside her. She felt suddenly shy, lying there with Nathan. "Do you know any of their names?" she asked, looking up at the sky.

Nathan groaned. "I can't think about stars right now." He reached for her.

"Nathan?"

"What?"

"I forgot to take my birth control pill."

"Can't you take it after?"

"I better take it now." And she crawled out from the tent. The pills were in her purse, and her purse was in the boat. But she needed the flashlight. It was down by the fire, in Nathan's pack.

With the flashlight off, she darted across the sand. The night air brushed her nakedness. She felt such freedom! She could see the boat's dark shape beyond.

Suddenly she was stepping through cold water. Alice switched on the flashlight, shining it at her feet. It was the tide, stealing in.

She had to wade out to the boat. The water was cold. Alice climbed in at the stern. She flicked the beam of the flashlight here and there. Where was her purse? She went forward and found her purse at the bow, in front of the engine box.

And under the foredeck, she found the totems.

The canvas no longer hid them. The canvas was now up on the beach, being used as a tent.

Alice moved the flashlight's beam over the greyed pieces of wood. Her heart pounded. What were they? The huge head of a raven caught the beam of light.

The carved wood was grey and cracked. The raven's beak was no longer sharp, but dull. And the bird's fierce, painted glare had also been worn away—by snow and rain and sun. With grey and blinded eyes, Raven stared up at her.

A chill ran down Alice's spine. She stood hunched and naked in the boat.

She moved the beam of light. The Sun was gazing up at her. It was an old grey face. It was not the Sun in his youth. The wood was cracked with deep lines. The claws of Old Age had scratched down his face. It was the spirit of the Sun that shone up at Alice. It was a tired spirit, but still burning strong.

What else had been hidden here, under the canvas, all this time? Hidden all through the fog across Hecate Strait. Hidden during that first night when the whaleboat trailed green fire in its wake. She and Nathan had lain together only inches away. She'd even leaned back against the canvas, against something hard underneath.

Anger now flared in Alice. The flashlight trembled in her hand. Its beam of light wavered. "Oh!" she cried aloud.

For here was the face of the storm. Alice was sure of it. The furious face of Scowling Frog glared up in the beam of light.

Alice backed up. She backed up, and then she turned, and climbed over the side of the whaleboat. She landed knee-deep in water. The tide was coming in fast. Alice didn't run up the beach. She tried to be calm. She knew that if she started to run she would scream. Instead she forced herself to a walk. She had the strange feeling that she was being followed. She crawled into the tent without a word.

"Alice, you're shaking." Nathan raised himself on one elbow. In the dark his fingers touched her cheek. She threw off his hand.

"Alice, what happened? Is Pozzi out there?"

"You're a thief."

"Oh god. You saw them." Nathan fell back.

"And you're a liar."

Alice lay without moving. "You almost got us all killed." Her heart pounded in her ears. Whatever it was that had followed her up the beach, at least she felt safer now. Even though she hated Nathan at this moment, she needed him.

But as her heart slowed in its pounding, she heard the strangest sound. It was coming from Nathan.

Alice tilted her head back where she lay. Out the end of the tent she could see the stars. The stars had always guided sailors. The stars helped sailors to know where they were, and where to go next in their journey.

She waited until Nathan had stopped crying. They lay in silence, side by side, looking up at the night sky. Quietly Alice asked, "Where do we go from here?"

It was a long time before Nathan answered. "I guess we go back. Take them back, to that old village."

Alice drew a deep breath. She turned to him. "That's what I hoped you'd say."

"Oh Alice, I'm sorry." Nathan pressed his face to her neck. She felt his wet cheeks on her skin. It had been so strange to hear him cry. The sound had come out so tight and thin. As if a man's sadness and guilt had to squeeze through such a narrow opening.

Nathan lifted his head. "Alice?"

She stared into the dark shadow that was his face. "What?"

"Will you let me make love to you?"

Alice closed her eyes to the stars.

"Yes."

Then she remembered her purse. It was still down in the boat. "Nathan…" she said between kisses. "The pill… I forgot to take it."

His mouth pressed at her ear. "What pill?"

*A*ll those who drown in the sea are not lost. If someone drowns, and someone on shore is sweeping the sea with a worried gaze, he is not lost. He is not lost if women and men and children lament, and pace the shoreline, and tear their hair with grief.

This goes on for days, for weeks. It goes on until the drowned man's totem is carved and painted, and raised high—where it can stare out to sea, to await his return.

7

BLACK LABEL

Through the hours, the stars had shifted in the sky. Nathan's head leaned next to Alice's as they gazed out from the tent.

"You know what I'd like?" said Alice. "I'd like a little of that whiskey, with some bread and cheese. How does that sound to you?"

"It sounds perfect." But Nathan made no move to get up. He wanted to stay right where he was—with Alice warm beside him. He drew a long, deep breath. The totems were going back. For the first time in days, Nathan felt light of heart.

Alice pointed to the sky, "What's that?"

"Which one?" He sighted along her arm.

"That star, right there," her finger pointing. "What's its name?"

"Alice," he answered.

"What."

"Alice—that's its name."

"Oh, you!" She turned her back to him.

Nathan planted kisses down her spine. "Will you forgive me?"

"Is that bottle of whiskey still in your pack?"

"All right. I'll go." Out of habit, Nathan put his glasses on, though it was still dark.

Alice called to him, "I just want to *try* the whiskey. See what it tastes like. And bring the food. Bring the whole pack, okay?"

"*Not so loud.*" The island was so small. He didn't want to wake Pozzi on the other side.

The fire had gone out. Only a single coal glowed red in the darkness. Nathan picked up his knapsack. The bottom of the knapsack was wet. "What the—" It was the tide. It had crept up higher than he'd figured. The sea lapped at the stones that circled the fire pit. Nathan could see the water now, a gleam along the sand.

Up at the tent, he handed in the pack. Alice sat up.

"Be careful, it's wet on the bottom."

Alice had the pack open. "There's no bottle in here."

"Let me look. Where's your flashlight?"

"Nathan, the bottle is gone."

They looked at each other in the dark tent. *Pozzi.* Pozzi had come back, after all.

Nathan pulled on his pants. "Hand me the flashlight."

"No, I'm coming with you."

"Dammit. He promised me. Pozzi gave me his word that he wouldn't drink on this trip."

Alice followed Nathan from the tent. "I wonder when he came

and took the bottle? Oh! Do you think he heard us—making love, I mean?" She thrust her arms into Nathan's big jacket, to cover her nakedness.

With high tide, the tiny island had shrunk. Only a narrow strip of sand circled the low hill. Nathan made his way through the scrub trees. He held Alice's hand tightly in his own. He played the flashlight over the ground.

"Pozzi?" Alice called.

They searched through the few trees. They walked down the other side of the shrunken island.

"Pozzi!" Nathan shouted, "Damn you, answer me!" He stopped for a moment to listen. He swung the flashlight's beam back and forth. Then his heart jumped. The light caught the gleam of glass. A glass bottle had been placed neatly on the top of a large rock. Even from this distance, Nathan knew what it was: Johnny Walker, Black Label. And the bottle looked empty.

Alice ran over and picked up the bottle. "It's not empty, Nathan. There's an inch of whiskey left."

"And the rest is swimming around in Pozzi's blood. He's here, somewhere. He's *got* to be here." Nathan swung the flashlight in a wide arc, past trees and rocks and sand. And water. Alice gave a cry.

It was Pozzi. His body floated in a bed of kelp. Kelp knobs bobbed in the water around him. Long streamers of kelp curled around his legs.

He must have fallen face down, and passed out on the beach. And the tide had crept up, to claim his feet, his legs, and one arm.

His other arm was flung above his head. Sand was his pillow. His lips were blue.

Alice waded in, she grabbed Pozzi by the arm. Nathan grabbed his other arm. As they dragged him up out of the water, green fire trailed in his wake. They dragged him far up onto dry sand.

"Let's turn him on his side." Nathan's voice sounded strangely high, even to himself.

Alice kneeled on the sand. She bent over and turned her ear to Pozzi's mouth. For a moment she didn't move. "He's breathing!"

The flashlight now lay on the sand, it shone into Pozzi's face. His chin was dark with stubble. His thin hair lay wet across his forehead. Nathan shook him. "You're a lucky man, Pozzi! Now wake up!"

But Pozzi didn't wake up.

"Nathan, we've got to take off his wet clothes. He's too cold. I think he's in shock." Alice fumbled at the laces of Pozzi's boots. "Oh, Pozzi, you crazy fool." Tears were in her voice.

Nathan began to undress the sodden man. "Damn you, Pozzi, don't you die. Don't you dare." He pulled at a wet shirt-sleeve. It caught at Pozzi's wrist, at the button. Nathan bit with his teeth at the cloth. He ripped the sleeve apart.

Alice had grabbed the flashlight.

"Where are you going?" Nathan called after her.

"To get our sleeping bag!"

Nathan eyes grew used to the darkness as he worked. Long streamers of kelp had wound themselves around Pozzi's legs. Nathan yanked at the kelp, tearing it away. He worked at the buckle of Pozzi's belt. He pulled it free. Pozzi lay on his back now. He was a big man, with plenty of flesh on him.

Pozzi lay stripped of clothes, of curses, of jokes. His pale, naked form lay heavy on the sand. In the darkness, Nathan bent close. "Don't worry, Pozzi," he whispered, "we'll get you warm."

Alice was back, gasping for breath, "I brought… I brought Pozzi's sleeping bag too."

She unrolled the bag onto the sand. She spread it open next to Pozzi's body. He was too heavy to lift, so they rolled him onto the sleeping bag.

"Oh Nathan, his skin is so cold."

Nathan was already pulling his own pants off. "Alice, take off that jacket, he's got to be next to our skin." Naked, Nathan lay down next to Pozzi. "Lie on the other side, Alice. Lie close."

They pulled the other sleeping bag over the three of them. And they shared with Pozzi their own warmth. They gave him back his life, as the tide withdrew, and the stars faded overhead.

Pozzi's snores woke Nathan. For a moment, he didn't know where he was. Then he remembered. He raised up on one elbow. "Alice?"

But Alice no longer lay on the other side of Pozzi. The sleeping bag had been carefully tucked in around the snoring man. And in the light of dawn, Alice was building a fire. She wore only the big jacket of red and black squares. Her legs were long beneath it. Her hair hung uncombed. She looked like a woman who had always lived in the wilds. Nathan watched her. It was as if he'd never seen her before. Alice broke a stick over her bare knee, and laid the pieces on the growing flames.

She'd hung Pozzi's wet clothes over bushes to dry. The torn sleeves of his shirt hung limp in the morning air.

Another snore snorted from Pozzi. The colour was back in his face. He looked terrible. But then, in the morning Pozzi always looked terrible.

Nathan pulled on his baggy pants. Barefoot, and bare-chested, he squatted down beside Alice's fire. His ribboned cap was still on the other side of the island, in the tent. So were his boots. He reached over and rubbed his hand up and down Alice's leg. The fire warmed his bare chest.

Birds flitted through the island's few trees. The sky was growing lighter. Nathan had slept for only a few hours, but he felt wide awake. Well-being filled him. He felt like giving thanks—for the morning, and for Alice. Even for Pozzi's snores.

Nathan reached up for Alice's hand. "Come and sit on my lap."

"I'm too heavy."

But she sat down. She pulled the jacket around her. "Have you changed your mind?"

Her question was for Nathan. But she stared over at Pozzi, who lay flat on his back, snoring loudly.

"Changed my mind about what, about you?"

"No. About taking the totems back."

"What do you think?"

She turned on his lap, to look at him. He waited while her eyes searched his face. She nodded. "Okay."

Pozzi slept most of the day. He lay across the bottom of the boat. Alice had to step over him every time she went forward. But most of the time she sat with Nathan at the stern. She was learning how to read a tide table, and how to steer. She learned that the left side of a boat was called the port side, and the right side was called the starboard.

There was another reason that Alice kept to the back of the boat. It wasn't so much that the Haida's totems scared her. It was that she could sense their power and weight at the bow. The canvas covered them. And she was glad for that. But she couldn't forget the strength in their grey, cracked faces.

Pozzi's head jerked forward on his chest to cough—and cough some more. Alice wondered if maybe he'd taken a little water into his lungs, after all. Then he fell back with a moan.

With the help of Alice and Nathan, Pozzi had managed to put on his own clothes. He'd climbed into the whaleboat—with Alice pulling and Nathan pushing. But now he could only snore, and cough, and roll his head back and forth. His wool cap was pulled down over his eyes.

"I'm glad I'm not him," said Alice.

"He's going to need coffee when he wakes up."

"I'm awake. When do we get to Alert Bay?" Pozzi's voice was a hoarse whisper. And it wasn't long before he was snoring again.

Alice thought of that empty bottle of whiskey. Pozzi had placed it carefully on the rock, for Nathan and her to find. He'd wanted them to see that it wasn't quite empty. There was an inch of whiskey left. Which meant that Pozzi was in control, Pozzi was no drunk. And he was polite—for hadn't he left some whiskey for them?

The next time Pozzi woke up, she would tell him that they'd passed Alert Bay hours ago.

"Pozzi, we're here, wake up." Alice lifted the wool cap from his face.

He blinked. "Too bright, too bright," he put a hand up to shade his eyes. "Where are we?"

"Campbell River," said Nathan. "We've got a hotel room."

They stopped at the first phone booth they came to. Nathan made the first call.

Alice stayed outside the booth. She leaned against the dusty glass. It was a collect call. To New York.

When calling collect, there was always that moment when you waited on the line. You waited to find out if the person at the other end would accept your call. In other words, pay for it.

"Hello, Dad." There was no door on the booth. Anyone passing on the street could hear Nathan talking to his father.

And then he was talking to his mother. Alice could tell by the change in his voice. She heard him speak her name, "Alice," into the phone. She turned around, and pressed both hands up against the glass. Nathan smiled out at her. He kept talking. He put his own hand up, and matched fingers with her as he talked.

Nathan hung up the phone, and stepped from the booth. "My father will wire me the money tomorrow."

"Did you tell him what you wanted it for?"

"He didn't ask." Nathan shook his head in wonder. "He just said he knew that I must really need it."

Nathan then bent down. "Pozzi? You want to call Grace and tell her you're all right?"

"Am I?" Pozzi sat on the curb. His elbows rested on his knees. He held his head with both hands, as if it might fall apart.

"Pozzi, now is your chance to call."

Alice spoke up. "Tell me Grace's number, Pozzi. I'll dial it for you."

But when it came time for Pozzi to take the phone, he shook his head. Alice made a face at him as she spoke into the receiver. "Hello. I'm a friend of Harry Pozzi's... No, not a girlfriend. Pozzi wants to speak with you." Alice stepped back from the booth. She stretched the phone cord as far as it would go. "Pozzi?" She held out the phone.

But Pozzi still sat slumped at the curb.

"Grace, he can't come to the phone right now, after all... Sure, I'll tell him." Alice held her hand over the phone. "Pozzi, Grace says she's sorry." Alice listened some more, and reported back to Pozzi. "She was just mad that you took off the way you did. That's why she tricked you."

Alice held the phone out again. "Pozzi! She wants to talk to you." Again, he shook his head.

"Grace, he can't. He's not feeling too well."

He lifted up his head. "How is she?"

"Pozzi wants to know how you are, Grace." Alice listened, and repeated what she heard to Pozzi. "There's no money in rotting totem poles."

At the curb, Pozzi nodded, as if he'd heard this before.

"She says to tell you that she doesn't have…" Alice plugged her other ear with her finger. "Grace, could you repeat that?"

Alice spoke slowly, for Pozzi to hear. "She's not sick. She just wanted to scare you…" Alice was looking down at Pozzi, who stared back at her. "Okay, Grace, I'll tell him. Yes. Goodbye."

Alice hung up. "She said to take care of your ulcer."

Pozzi rose to his feet. "She's not sick? She doesn't have cancer? You mean she lied to me?"

Alice poked his shoulder. "Come on. Let's go get clean."

The three of them walked down the street. Alice listened with half an ear to the string of curses coming from Pozzi. She smiled to herself: they must look a pretty sight. Her own jeans were stained and dirty. Pozzi's sleeves hung in rags from his arms. And Nathan's old green sweater had new holes in it.

Their hotel room smelled of stale cigarette smoke. One large bed took up most of the space. "Ladies first," said Pozzi, with a bow towards the bathroom's shower.

"No, you first," Alice gave him a little push. "You need it even more than I do."

Nathan handed Pozzi his bag. He set his own pack on the bed next to Alice's suitcase. "Don't use up all the hot water," he called to Pozzi.

"And hurry up," called Alice.

Pozzi was slow. Finally, he emerged from the bathroom. His

eyes were still bloodshot, but his cheeks were clean and shaved. He held his arms out in front of him. "I just now noticed. What happened to my shirt? I don't remember my sleeves being all torn like this."

Nathan laughed. "Just roll them up, Pozzi."

Alice took her suitcase into the bathroom and closed the door. She rubbed steam from the mirror. She rubbed a circle clear and saw her face for the first time in days.

It was a stranger's face that looked back at her. The stranger's mouth was bare of lipstick. Her skin was brown from the sun. There was soot on her nose. And her dark eyes shone clear and bright… Alice heard a knock. "It's Nathan. May I come in?" And the stranger smiled.

Pozzi sat on the edge of the big bed. His head was clearer now. And the truth was sinking in. Grace wasn't going to die. He took a deep breath. Grace was going to live. He let out a long sigh of relief. He didn't have to marry her.

Pozzi's fingers trembled as he rolled a cigarette. He felt as if his whole being had been broken into a hundred pieces. Someone had glued him back together while he'd slept, but the pieces were mixed up. Even so, he felt better than he had an hour ago. Under the hot water of the shower, he'd washed most of the shame away.

He didn't light the cigarette. He put it in his shirt pocket. He could hear muffled laughter from behind the bathroom door. He couldn't help but listen. He bent his head and stared down at his shoes. Why fool himself? A girl like Alice—what would she want with a man like him? A man who'd been broken and mended so many times.

He twisted his head towards the window. Outside, there were buildings and telephone wires. Store signs blinked on and off. This was real life. This was the real world. And sitting on the bed, looking out the window, Pozzi longed for the lost world. The world of dark forests, and of deer that leapt across your path. A world where tall grey totem poles leaned like old drunks. Like himself. Pozzi stood up from the bed. He pulled the curtain closed. The light hurt his eyes.

He fished in his pocket for the cigarette.

He was still coughing when Alice and Nathan came out of the bathroom. Alice was drying her hair with a towel. Pozzi couldn't take his eyes off her. She was wearing her blue dress. She was trying to torture him.

Nathan's beard was wet, and he smelled of soap. Pozzi looked him over. "Hey kid—have we ever been this clean?"

"Pozzi, we have to talk." Nathan leaned against the wall. He cleaned his glasses on his sweater then put them back on. The thick glass made his eyes seem larger. He looked straight at Pozzi. "I'm taking the totems back."

"What do you mean? Back where?"

"To the Queen Charlottes."

Pozzi's throat tightened. His thoughts jerked here and there. He shook his head, to shake free of Nathan's words. But he knew they were fact. He jumped up, pacing the small room. "You expect me to get back into that boat and cross the Strait again?"

Nathan spoke softly. "Pozzi, there's a bus leaving at four this afternoon, going down-island to Victoria. From there, you can take the ferry to Seattle."

"You're crazy! Why give up now? We can get a lot of money from those totems!" Pozzi stopped in his pacing. "But I forget, you don't care about money—not a rich kid like you." The moment those words were out of Pozzi's mouth, he wished he could take them back.

"Pozzi, I'm broke, and you know it."

"I'm sorry, kid, sorry. I just got excited." Pozzi sat down heavily on the bed. "Phew… I feel kinda lightheaded." He closed his eyes for a moment.

"You just need food." It was Alice speaking. "We all need food." Sweet Alice. What was she doing? She'd taken his hand. "Pozzi, here's money for the bus and the ferry."

He looked down at the Canadian bills she'd placed in his hand. The $50 bills were coloured red, and carried a likeness of the Queen's unsmiling face.

It took Pozzi a moment to compose himself. But when he finally looked up at Alice, it was with a grin. "You sure this isn't play money?"

Pozzi leaned back, he turned his face up to the warm sun. His thin hair was combed back from his high forehead. So… tomorrow he would see Grace. And he didn't have to get back into that damn boat.

The three of them waited on the bench in front of the bus

station. Nathan sat on one side of Pozzi, and Alice on the other side, in her blue dress.

"What time is it, Pozzi?"

He drew his watch from his pocket. He looked at its face circled with numbers, but his thoughts were elsewhere. "You know, I can't remember much about last night, on that island. It's like a blackout." He poked Nathan with his elbow, "I guess that's never happened to you, hey kid?

"You almost died, Pozzi, from cold."

"I did, really? I don't remember being cold. What I *do* remember is being warm." Pozzi's voice softened. "It was like a dream. I thought I'd died and gone to heaven… I *knew* I was in heaven," Pozzi grinned, his gold tooth gleaming, "because two bare-naked women lay down next to me, one on each side, real close."

Pozzi looked down at his watch. "What? What are you two laughing at? The time is 10 minutes to four."